DIVING INTO DEEP WATER

DIVING INTO DEEP WATER

2-minute plunges for time-poor literary lovers

Narelle Fernance
D'Arcy Lloyd
Barbara Maxwell
Chris McIntosh
Kris Nissam
Brydie O'Shea
Anna Russell

Foreword by Michael Burge

High Country BOOKS

First published in Australia 2025 by High Country Books
An imprint of The Makers Shed www.themakersshed.org

ISBN: 9780645270570

A catalogue record for this
book is available from the
National Library of Australia

Contents

Foreword

THE HIGH COUNTRY Writers group is an informal gathering of wordsmiths who started meeting at The Makers Shed, a small corrugated-iron shop at the southern end of the high street of Glen Innes in northern inland New South Wales, in mid-2019.

In 2024, the group moved with that business to a century-old former butcher shop on the New England Highway at Deepwater, at the heart of the traditional lands of the Ngarrabul people.

Participants from Glen Innes, Inverell, Bingara, Grafton, Ashford and Deepwater regularly discussed the art of writing until one member – Anna Russell – suggested the group start to write 300-word responses to a prompt, one word or a short phrase selected at random from the High Country Books shelves in the lounge area where we meet.

This 'homework' was then read out to the group at the next session, leading to many wonderful listening experiences for all those within earshot.

Somewhere along the line, High Country Books decided these moments were too good to leave hanging invisible in the air, and offered to publish the work with each writer's permission.

This collection has been minimally edited, preserving each writer's response to every prompt (which appear as chapter headings), and their writing style. The 13 prompts appear in order of them being set, but there is no strict order to the 300-word stories within the chapters, I have simply curated them by feel so that readers can enjoy the way the literary responses vary so widely.

The result captures an incredible breadth of storytelling which the writers workshopped into the promotional materials for this collection, sessions that were guided by D'Arcy Lloyd.

High Country Books is delighted that the group developed a title with more than one meaning. *Diving Into Deep Water* is both a reference to the township where The Makers Shed operates, and the act of creative courage that these writers threw themselves into.

That level of personal bravery is what our artisanal business is all about: creating despite the odds of success, regardless of opinions and in collaboration with like-minded artists.

I thoroughly commend all these stories to you and encourage you to embrace the third meaning of this collection's title, which is all about you, the reader, experiencing the depths of writers' imaginations when handed a theme and asked to explore the infinite within such a disciplined word count.

On that note, let me fill you in on the various "rules" of this project and how some were broken, of course!

Any reader counting words will find the odd infraction of the group agreement, but none of the contributors thought this should be cause for any culling.

Not every writer wrote to every prompt. Hey, life gets busy and you can't do everything! Some wrote more than one response to a prompt. Let's not discourage them!

Not every prompt was extracted from another piece of writing. Some were specific challenges: to write without using the letter E

('Sans E'), to pen a short autobiography ('Memoir') and the account of someone else, from biological or chosen family ('Biography').

Some of the works are part of larger storytelling projects, details of which you'll find in the author biographies at the back of this book; but the vast majority are standalone pieces.

Between these covers you'll find multiple genres: crime, horror, historical fiction, humour, fantasy, poetry, experimental fiction and non-fiction. Some may find themes and terms they find offensive, used in historical context or otherwise. There is no content warning apart from this advice: skip any parts you find challenging, but don't let a little literature scare you!

Thanks to all the participants who contributed their work, and to those who took on leadership roles at key times of this process, facilitating sessions and keeping the project moving along. Kris Nissam and D'Arcy Lloyd put their hands up for proofreading; Brydie O'Shea hosted a session at her beautiful garden, and Deepwater's Top Pub made our group welcome while The Makers Shed was being renovated.

Big gratitude to all the writers for entrusting their work to an emergent publisher. As an acknowledgement of their contribution, High Country Books at The Makers Shed will donate ten per cent of all sales of *Diving Into Deep Water* to our region's Westpac Rescue Helicopter Service, for as long as the title is in print.

Dive in … and keep an eye out for our other titles!

– Michael Burge

Filing Cabinet

In the Undergrowth
by Chris McIntosh

HE NOTICED THE smell before he caught sight of the unusual shape, the angular beige box out-of-place amongst the tree ferns and undergrowth. As he crept closer, stepping cautiously over rocks and ground cover, he also recognised the busy drone of hungry flies.

The metal office filing cabinet lay on its side, facing down the slope. He stopped next to it – his hand over his mouth in a futile attempt to stifle the putrid taste – and looked critically over the scene. The style of cabinet was familiar to him, just like the one in his own home office. The grass around it had been flattened, but some creepers had cast thin green tendrils up the sides and curled their way into the gaps around the drawers. How long had it been here? A week? Two?

The cabinet itself didn't seem to be damaged at all. He glanced up towards the gravel fire trail but couldn't even see it through the scrub. The regrowth from the bushfires a couple of years ago was thick. Whoever had dumped the cabinet here hadn't simply rolled it down the hill – it had been carried here.

'Ooooh ... this is not good,' he muttered.

Sunlight glinted off a shiny silver key in the lock above the top drawer.

In his mind he heard some gruff detective shouting, 'Who's been contaminating my crime scene!?' He also feared what he might find inside. He knew he shouldn't open the drawer. Absolutely not.

He reached for the key and turned it.

As the lock disengaged the top drawer thumped, then rolled open. It stopped hard and something the size of a football spilled out onto the grass and leaves, coming to rest near his feet. The eyes of the thing were half-shut and sunken, the swollen brown tongue protruding from a gaping mouth, but the features were unmistakable. He realised, in horror, that he was looking down at his own severed head.

He screamed, but there was no sound. Somewhere nearby a bellbird sang, and the tendrils that would one day bury the cabinet rustled gently in the breeze.

Oh, Mr Wilson

by Anna Russell

I STARTED WORKING for Wilson & Pratt straight out of secretarial college, first as office junior and then I was promoted to the typing pool, when Miss Stephens left to get married. Old Mr Wilson didn't like married girls working there, he said that marriage was too distracting.

Five years later I became Mr Wilson's secretary as Miss Plume, who'd worked for him for twenty-seven years, had had a stroke and was pensioned-off. We knocked along quite well as long as I managed to avoid the bottom patting or shoulder squeezing he was so fond of.

One week, Mr Wilson was away and the articled clerk asked me for a file so he could deal with a client. I couldn't find it anywhere, which was strange as I was careful with my filing. In the last filing cabinet drawer I found a folder marked personal, which when I lifted it out, spilled a pile of photographs onto the floor.

I stood startled by the top image. It was of me from behind, bending over to put something in the filing cabinet, my bottom sticking out. I pushed the photo aside with a finger to see if they were all of me and some were, but the others were of glamorous Miss Pride standing on a step stool to get a book from a high shelf and showing her stocking tops, and sweet Miss Francis leaning forward over her desk, her blouse front gaping.

How had he taken them, and what should I do? I wasn't going to lose my job over this. I grabbed a manila envelope and jammed the photos into it, before putting it in my bag. Then I put the folder back where I'd found it and closed the drawer. It wasn't as if he could ask me where the pictures had gone.

Lost Documents

by Narelle Fernance

TWO MEN FACED-OFF across the wooden filing cabinet in the corner of Uralla Police Station. It was a cold July afternoon in 1871. Senior Superintendent Martin Quigley eyed the local officer-in-charge, Superintendent Stan Brown, with a crippling stare.

'What do you mean that **THIS** is the Thunderbolt file? What the hell am I to believe? That these few documents represent all there is to know about the infamous bushranger purported to have plagued the Northern Tablelands? The nobs in Macquarie Street have been talking about how this ruffian has been robbing citizens, then riding off into the mountains with nary a challenge.'

'But, but …' Brown started to stutter, drawing himself up to his full height, and squaring his chest, as he did his best to recover from the tirade.

'So, where are the other documents? The witness accounts? The identification by young Monckton?' continued Quigley. 'Locals who knew Fred Ward have been quite adamant that the body was not that of Fred Ward. Popular opinion is that the body was his uncle, Harry Ward, an impostor.'

'I met Fred, back in the early '50's,' Quigley pointed out, 'before the law enforcers made a bushranger of him. Then again in '67 when he and his little wife bailed-up my coach. Personally, I would have to wonder whether the easy-on-the-eye horseman that I knew, could ever look anything like the photo or the corpse displayed at Blanche's Inn after the shooting.'

By then Brown had recovered enough to slam the filing cabinet shut with timber shattering force.

'What does it matter which "corn-stork" it is? Surely these second-generation colonist are all layabouts. Who cares whether it was Fred Ward, or Harry Ward?' he added at a roar, glaring back at his superior.

To Brown's amazement, Quigley just turned to cover the amused grin on his face, and headed for the door. The early swirls of fog whipped up by the evening wind rose as he stepped out into the street. His hand tapped his pocket holding the secondment papers signed by Henry Parkes. Quigley mused that Fred would now be in California. The ex-bushranger's skills with horses would have given him a reputation. He would be easy to find!

The Cherub Killer

by Brydie O'Shea

I FINISHED THE brief on the Cherub Killer, while Ellie played with dolls on the detective's room floor. Not my normal M.O. (I don't hold with bringing kids to work), but Craig had the boys at Under-9s Rugby and Ellie was – well, just a child. So here she was in Mummy's office oblivious to the flurry of arrests and charges going on in other parts of the building. Preening her Barbie Fashionistas, Ellie was seven going on seventeen. She styled her hair to match her dolls; even chose dresses that looked Mattel.

'I *luv* you Barbie,' Ellie said, 'and I *luuuv* you too, other Barbie.'

She had six in total (I know – spoilt), but Ellie treated them like people, smoothing their clothes, tucking in shirts. She was such a little mother. I watched her from my desk feeling love so tangible, it hurt.

Not so my feelings toward John Blaney; dubbed the Cherub Killer. Blaney targeted innocent children, luring them with sweets and toys, only to rape and kill them – decapitating and preserving their heads.

Was it trophy keeping? Or to hamper identification? (I would never know those answers now since Blaney was murdered by fellow inmates at Long Bay).

I cut string and tied the wad of documents. Put scissors down then locked Blaney's evidence in the filing cabinet drawer.

Turning to Ellie I said, 'Mummy's going out for a second, Angel.'

She looked up, smiled then returned to Barbie.

I was less than five minutes, but I swear my heart stopped upon return.

Ellie stood upright, scissors in hand. None of her Barbies had heads. They'd been cut off and tears wet Ellie's baby blues. Pointing at the filing cabinet, she tonelessly spoke. 'Blaaynee said, "Do it Ellie! Or I'll chop your head off next".'

The A-Z of Life
by Kris Nissam

ACTIVE EVERY DAY, some days harder than others. Attitude is nine-tenths of the law.

Beautiful sunrise, sunset, cool mornings, waves crashing, starlit nights where I see my family.

Caring for animals, people and the environment. Only when earned and/or deserved.

Dedicated to the lifestyle and those who choose to share in it.

Enthusiastic about life in general, the more hard knocks the more appreciative you become.

Funny outlook even in the most dire of situations.

Grateful for fresh air and water and for the food that I eat.

Happy most of the time, but sadness and grief have their place too.

Independent to a fault. Taurean star sign, stubborn too.

Joyful when you pull off a stunt, see a shooting star or an event is successful.

Kind to many, returned by few. C'est la vie

Laughing makes you feel better, so does crying too.

Mindful in every aspect of life and hopefully respectful to all.

Naughty but nice, sometimes it's great to be wicked!

Opportunistic, seize the day. Carpe diem. Take the chances ignore the glances.

Patient in so many aspects of life and loving.

Quiet in my solitude and life on the farm and very happy to be so.

Reserved in many social situations, outrageous in others.

Silent contemplation each evening on the achievements or disasters of the day.

Tested to the limit quite often; this only strengthens one's resolve, ideas and core beliefs.

Understanding of the hierarchy of needs for all, food, water, shelter, love.

Veering off the beaten path, whoops, but what an adventure!

Watchful, waiting, whistling in the morning.

Xanadu, a place of idyllic magnificence wherever that is for you. Snowcapped mountains or crashing waves on the beach.

Yippee a new day!

Zzzzzzzzz sleeping peacefully.

Heavy Metal Deadline

by D'Arcy Lloyd

HE HAS THREE minutes! Tick tock!

'Downstairs' – the print men are pacing around mammoth presses richly primed with the broadsheet's one hundred pages; bar page one. *Breaking!*

'Upstairs' – colleagues and editors, in-chief and of-staff – are alert and mute but keeping their distance. The fireball journo monsters the typewriter's keys. Dot, click, clack, whirr – repeat – repeat, until … nothing.

Finished? No!

A crack is shattering silence. His typewriter, with shackled power cord in flailing strangulous pursuit, careens murderously across the room. Horrified colleagues hit the deck to a chorus of profanities.

Disconnected from the gravity of his actions, he's plundered a colleague's machine, filled the chamber with the crumpled story and monstering again!

The Chiefs are huddling in private, eyes fixed on him – The Perpetrator.

Meanwhile, having barely missed a colleague's head, the Reject has collided full thrust with an ancient mongrel filing cabinet. At eight times the weight of IBM, it could be a David-and-Goliath battle. Still … twenty-two kilos hitting anything at any velocity has to kick. Has it what!

In magnificent retaliation, Filing Cabinet's loins are awakened and she's wailing a battle cry from her top drawer. The rollout is balletic, her tune one of excruciating caterwauls as loose files atop vomit across the room. She's landed, rocked, rolled and spewed some more, while IBM's golf-ball whizzes his sad sinless death throw. His morbid nicotine stench peppers the room.

The sloppy-suited journo rips copy from the chamber and thunders, 'Boy-y-y-y! Tick tock! Tick tock!' Though quivering, the copy boy will break his record side-vaulting down six flights.

The Chief has sidled to his desk and commands – forebodingly – 'My office!'

Filing Cabinet impossibly casts a triumphant smile.

The building rumbles its bedtime tune.

Here is the news!

Filing Cabinet impossibly casts a triumphant smile.

The building rumbles its bedtime tune.

Quiet Observer

My Observation of Life as it Happens
by Kris Nissam

SO, AS I sit in my office, looking out over the peaceful paddocks, I hear the highway behind me, full of rush and hurry. Roaring motors, the flap of flat tyres, the friendly toot to a neighbour, the screech of brakes. Bloody kangaroos! Barking dogs in cattle truck boxes and the early morning garbage truck lift, drop and bang.

I am appreciating my solitude, my farming practises, and my observation of life.

Each day I watch my herd of Brahmans and note what the play of the day is. Little calves on top of the mound are the King or Queen of the day, unless pushed aside by a stronger opponent. (Reminds me of working life.)

The mob roams freely and selectively grazes, choosing the sweet and dry grasses. Food miles are minimal and the seasonal availability is what they choose to eat. I also choose to follow this way of eating, enjoying the seasonality of fresh fruit and vegetables and home-grown unstressed meat.

I watch the dogs play, tumble and bark at any movement near the farm.

I'm also protective of my space after a working life so full of people. I love roaming to the river to sit peacefully and contemplate.

The scenery varies with the wind and the weather the heat and the cold. The changing of the seasons and phases of the moon all offer the availability of differing activities. Moon baking or swimming, fire lighting and cooking.

No charge, no rules, no team playing.

The personalities of all the animals, including the wildlife, are a constant joy and form of entertainment. They all have a home here.

Similar view to people really. You don't keep a biting dog or kicking horse. Hence many have been evicted from my inner circle.

A wise person stays silent, observing the rhetoric of others.

Home

by Barbara Maxwell

I WAS SURE I'd seen it, maybe I was wrong, but I needed to see it.

I had not been able to do this in so long, but now I was free and I had the opportunity, I just had to do it. I paced a little as I thought about it, what could I do, how to approach this. I knew that what was about my neck would make a difference, it still hurt, the memory was not going away, ever, but there were other memories there as well. They were different, there was warmth, I remember, and I'd always felt so, well, comfortable, but it was a long time ago. That is how it seemed to me. I was so lost for so very long and then it had happened. I could never forget that hurt.

I looked again. I was becoming sure of what I had seen. It was that warmth, not the hurt. Quietly, a little closer, I'd see better. My legs, so tired, and I was sore, it had been such a struggle, now I had to decide. Such fear I'd felt but I just had that memory of warmth, comfort. I could see things as they'd been, in my head it was there, and the children, I remembered now as I got closer, the noises, the laughter, the running.

Was it the same?

I looked again. It was so close now, and there was another person, bigger than the laughing ones. Yes, I had to do it, something had drawn me here, I know it, I know this place.

I crept forward, then they saw me. The little people made noises to the other person who looked up and saw me and stared.

Bruce, Bruce, I heard my name. I knew that voice, I barked and ran, I felt the warmth and comfort again before I even reached them, I was home.

Planted

by Anna Russell

CRESSIDA HATED GOING to the dentist, not because of the pain but because of that feeling of being trapped, of being smothered. She told Noel, an older man in the art department about this and Noel said, 'I can help you with that.' He said he was a qualified hypnotherapist, he even showed her his card, and he promised to teach her self hypnosis.

That evening, when everyone had gone, they went to the boss's office. Cressida sat in a leather armchair with wide arms and Noel sat in front of her in a smaller chair. He put his hand on her knee and told her to count back from one hundred. When she came to, Noel was standing looking down on her. He said he had made a suggestion to her subconscious which she could call on later. He told her to repeat to herself, I am calm, I can breathe, I feel no pain, and if this didn't work, to tap her knee which would activate the subconscious.

As Cressida and her friend Cassie were walking to work on the Monday, they passed a church-like building and on the front door was a poster with a book cover on it, L. Ron Hubbard, *Dianetics.*

Cressida said, 'That's weird, that book's on Noel's desk.'

Cassie looked at her and said, 'Stay away from that stuff, it's creepy.'

Tuesday, dentist day. Cress said she didn't want anaesthetic; she was going to try self-hypnosis.

The dentist said, 'Okay but raise your arm if you feel uncomfortable.'

It went well for a while, as she repeated to herself, 'I am calm, I can breathe, I feel no pain,' then she started to panic. She urgently tapped her knee and immediately had the sensation of a hand sliding under her skirt, so she raised her hand to stop the work.

An Opportunity to Savour

by Narelle Fernance

TO SAY SHE was a quiet observer could be correct, but Francesca was more than that. She had served them coffee and delicacies on the veranda, and discerned that their yarning on common experiences indicated a trusting friendship. But just now, Fred Ward had shown clear animosity when Sam Reilley had spoken to her. Perhaps one could interpret the comments as innocent flirting – but surely, just complimenting her cooking, and neat appearance in her housekeeper's uniform, was more likely polite comment.

Her employer, Fred, had always conducted himself in a professional manner in relation to their living arrangement. He conducted his farming business from home, and she attended to the housework and cooking. Generally he lived a simple life, with just the occasional dinner party for his friends or business associates. So her responsibilities were not onerous, and the relationship was one of mutual respect.

But this morning something had changed. Sam, a neighbour, had returned after last night's party to continue a conversation on a matter that the two men had discussed during the party. The conversation seemed to be benign enough – something about how Sam might apply for membership of the Turf Club committee. He was clearly enthused about his ideas to progress the thinking of the board.

So the flash-point could not be in relation to their discussion. Francesca had to contemplate that perhaps Fred did not like Sam paying her attention. Why should Fred object? He had no designs on her affections, or so she had always thought! She had given him no encouragement to change that mindset, but could it be that simple; that Fred, for whatever reason, was beginning to think otherwise?

No, Francesca was not just a silent observer, but rather, one experiencing awareness of new possibilities!

Abe's Lament

by D'Arcy Lloyd

I WAS NOT the first alumni. Fifteen came before. Thirty-one have followed. Naturally, that number must grow, though I grieve for our republic's parlous state and future.

Coincidentally, it is one-hundred-and-fifty-eight years since my last breath. Though captive for a tad over a century in this gigantic marbled-state, I am well-situated to have not ceased from observing and reflecting. Fortunate now – for just three precious minutes – my voice is *liberated*.

Lauded as the Great Emancipator, I once rather stridently asserted, 'I would rather be assassinated than surrender the Declaration's principles.' I might have added, 'No, no, only joking!' specifically to Mr Wilkes-Booth who presumed putting a bullet through the brain of just one man would arrest Emancipation.

Inscribed behind, to my left, is my Second Inauguration speech. Noting now, 'With malice toward none, and charity for all,' would perhaps have been better qualified with, 'excluding the unhinged.'

You see how satirical wit has steadfastly remained my loyal companion beyond life.

Now, this precious brief gift charges me to leave you with a challenge. Oh, that I could be prideful for those youthful warnings I detailed, at just 28. I cannot but must urgently flag just a fraction of sentiment I expressed in *The Perpetuation of Our Political Institutions*.

Its final impossibly prophetic words – truncated and modernised now – called for, inter alia – our reverence for the Republic's Constitution and laws lest we suffer maniacal ambition-driven 'mobocratic' forces 'to the last trump'. Oh yes, *trump!*

I affirm that my final words – but two – were prophetic for, 'the gates of hell have prevailed against' our political institution.

Time for quiet, farewell friends,

Abe!

The Memory of Anne

by Chris McIntosh

SHE HAD TO admit that being dead had its advantages. Since she'd died she hadn't had to worry about her diet, exercise, getting enough sleep or any of the countless things that might make her sick (again). She could go anywhere she wanted, any time, without even thinking about the price of fuel or flights. No stubbing her toe on coffee tables, no bad hair days, no telemarketers, no hot flushes.

Of course there were downsides too. Not having a brain made it difficult to remember things. Anne sometimes wished people could hear her contributions to their conversations. She was sure they'd value her newfound insight and wisdom. Then there were the animals: for some reason they all seemed to be quite disturbed by her. Cats would growl, dogs whimper and horses bolt any time she was near. Having been an animal lover when she was alive, this often made her sad.

Tonight she wasn't sad though; she was delighted. Her son Philip had recently met a lovely young woman (a little too young, in Anne's opinion, but that seemed to be the way of things). He'd invited her around for dinner and everything went rather well. Anne had spent the night perched on one end of the couch, ghost knitting. She'd admired Phil's efforts in the kitchen – even if the results were mixed – rolled her non-existent eyes at her dear boy's terrible jokes and chuckled at his clumsy attempts at flirting. Late in the night when Phil walked his date to the front door, Anne had retired to the kitchen, to give them some privacy – old habits really did die hard.

It was quite a while before she heard the door close and Phil returned to the kitchen, Cheshire Cat grin and sparkling eyes. He slowly leaned back against the counter and for a long time just smiled stupidly at the fridge. What Anne would have given to be able to talk to him now. Eventually he did speak, softly.

'Wish you were still here, Mum. You would have liked her.'

I Like to Watch

by Brydie O'Shea

I HID AND waited in my spot by the river. I knew the dry heat would bring people out and I did not bide long before a girl approached.

I smelt her before I saw her, deodorant mixed with the eucalyptus oil of the woodlands, so I hunkered down in leaf litter and watched her come into view. She was larger than my usual victims, which made me wary as I am not like the other predators. They stalk, or downright chase. But I am a quiet observer. I ambush. I like to watch.

The girl came close; within arm's distance and started to undress. I do not know what thrilled me most, her flawless teen skin, or the fact she did not sense her danger. Even then I did not attack. I play the waiting game. I had been waiting there for days and would not strike 'til I was absolutely trophy-sure. She seemed distracted; possibly thinking of cool mud beneath her feet and fresh water on her face while I checked, and double checked. She was indeed alone but would fight unless I caught her completely unaware.

She placed her bag beside me, and I admit I was high on being the king of camouflage. If she had seen me, she would never mistake me (all stocky and stumpy and coiled), but she never had a chance. I did not need to lure her. My red and black bands blended so perfectly, that she knew no reason not to sit against my arrowed head.

Then I struck. With lightning speed. My enormous fangs injected toxic venom in her hand. This was no warning; this was the kill bite. Too late she realised her peril and seconds before paralysis she screamed my name.

'Death Adder.'

Dangled Mid-air

The Last Heist

by Narelle Fernance

THE WORDS DANGLED mid-air between us! I twisted around in the saddle to follow his gaze. He stepped down from the coach and repeated his statement:

'Perhaps you should abandon this particular heist, eh?' he said, eyebrows raised a little more in emphasis.

I was now starting to panic as I realised how sick my darling Sunday, my partner in crime, really was. She sat huddled, as she shivered, barely clinging to her mount. My pet name for her was "Sunday" but she was my wife, Mary Ann. I momentarily forgot our plan to hold up the Mudgee Cobb and Co Mail Coach – and the fact that I had realised the passengers therein, were none other than Inspector of Police, Martin Quigley and his wife. I had come across Quigley on earlier occasions, before and during my "career" as "Captain Thunderbolt", bushranger of the New England. Therefore I knew him to be a Trap with unusual understanding and sympathy for the underdog. But I had no illusions about the present situation, in which Sunday and I found ourselves.

Bloodstained saliva trickled from Sunday's beautiful mouth as her shoulders heaved with each deadly coughing fit. The insidious

Consumption, that she had inherited from the cold damp Maitland Prison cells, was ready to claim her. The heavy early morning fog and biting cold served to hasten that reality to us all.

Sunday's revolver had been pointing at the coach driver, while mine had been trained on the coach doorway. However, it was obvious Quigley was not feeling threatened. He knew that I never carried a loaded gun and therefore had not killed anyone in my efforts to coerce the rich, and sometimes the poor, to hand over their money and jewellery.

'Yes, I think it wise that you forget this one,' Quigley confirmed, handing me a small book containing several five pound notes! He nodded and climbed back into the coach!

When You Came Back to Me
by Brydie O'Shea

When you came back to me
I found out part of you didn't.
I think you wanted to tell me
About Vietnam
(You said we had history
And that I had an easy ear),
But when you tried
your words lost thrust
And dangled mid-air
(Like you were parachuting
to the drop zone at Nui Dat).

You stayed quiet.

(I missed your in-depth take on life).

I wanted to help you find your voice

(Because I wanted you)

But a piece of you stayed in the jungle.

Still with Golf Company.

Communicating silently

Pulling the fishing-line string

Across the foxholes

Of your patrol.

You were lost to me

In the maze of your mind.

Outsmarting Viet Cong

In our bed.

Your moans were real

Though not of 'us'

And you were

Stuck.

Unseen in tiger stripes

On olive-drab greens

Traipsing The Horseshoe

Out from SAS Hill.

Somewhere in another parallel

We swim laps at the sea.

You take your shoes off

And climb rocks
And talk of crossing
Suspension bridges in Nepal.
Those were your dreams.
But not now –
On dark you dream
To bridge the span
To find your
Misplaced signalman.

I loved your all
But you were not
All here to
Love.
You lived in
Shadows
Of your prior self.
And I wished
For you and I
That you would find
Your missing core.

Instead, you dangled
By rope
Mid-air
Between the ceiling
And the floor.

Risky Business

by D'Arcy Lloyd

THE REDOLENT FEAR oozes beneath the boardroom's doors. Barring a sliver of space at one end, the room looks corpulent!

A solid mix of women and men from the corporate suite create a tessellated plotline around the Board table. The full complement of forty, including shareholders, lines the walls for this Extraordinary General Meeting.

Beyond the boardroom, an absurd and dubious cast of conceited advisors lines the corridor's walls. The "boardroom" desperately fearfully wants to know why! Their texts would testify to swarms of paranoid messaging, though none comes close to the facts.

The respected no-nonsense Managing Director enters. Restrained smiles are offered and returned. She taps the lectern and waves her mobile to signal phones off. The Chairman's door opens, and the Board enters, unusually, ahead of the Chairman.

As womens' smiles dissolve in seconds, mens' nostrils expand and contract. Fetid air gushes forth.

The Chairman's ever present disdainful visage is oddly absent. Disquiet compounds. His mere threatening presence elicits forty swords a-dangling mid-air like an armada of Dionysus's warnings to Damocles.

As infamous urgency and bombast dissolve, he falteringly delivers two thunderbolts that stun the room. Early retirement! The inexplicable gifting of his enormous shareholding to everyone present! Suspicion is palpable.

The room lights up with flashes from a dozen phones defiantly left on. Screens announce breaking news that *their* Jekyll-and-Hyde chairman faces multiple counts of bullying and harassment.

Exposed at last, the Chair's eyes hover at the cavernous room's epicentre. The French might say *suspendre* – in space, time, and expectations. The MD's poker-face flickers with restrained triumph. The scene is tragic, yet no one cries laughs breathes.

The chairman's prepared speech flutters to the floor. With head bowed, forty glistening swords escort his pathetic retreat.

The room twitters. The air freshens.

Four Poems

by Kris Nissam

Underwear

Driving into town, with the window down
Fresh air, not a care
Until I saw the underwear!
Dangled mid-air on the line
More prominent than any sign
Higher than a six-foot fence
To me it seemed a little dense
It could've been wound down of course
Using that handle on the side of the hoist
But no! Just a brazen midair display
Next time I'll drive another way.

Galahs

It's raining, the class called
And they all ran to see
What the fuss was about
Oh, what could it be?
One hundred galahs, dangled mid-air in a tree
Upside down, enjoying a shower for free.

Hills Hoist

The old hills hoist had seen its day
We had to go the modern way
Bits of plastic and steel tubing
About that there'll be no musing
The old hills hoist is a tradition,
served its purpose, completed its mission
Years of service tall and true
Drying clothes for me and you

Nappies dangled mid-air on-line
Announced the arrival of kids on time
Cold wet washing, dripping for days
Yes, they were 'The good old days'

But today, kids are this hoist's demolition
Go dangle mid-air, it's a competition
To see who can finally trash the line

Have fun, swing around and enjoy this time
The laughter, the swinging
The hills hoist demise
Left us all smiling with tears in our eyes.

Red Setter

The red setter full of life and exuberance
Ran too quickly, without any sense
Over the cliff and down into the scrub
Then curled up like a baby cub

Only one way to rescue my dog
Off with the sarong and anchor to a log
Hold my ankles while I dangle midair
Wearing only my underwear

Loop the sarong, right around his middle
Right about now I could do with a piddle
But this job isn't quite done yet
We need some super-human strength

I'll pull the dog while you pull me
Adrenaline pumping in all three
Rescue mission completed successfully!

High Notes

by Chris McIntosh

NOBODY SAW IT appear, or admitted knowing how it got there, but the piano floating several metres above the main street was quite real. The local kids had proved that – first with some gravel scraped out of the gutter, then with someone's cricket ball. The ball had broken off a piece of decorative timber moulding from the front, a piece of timber that the town pharmacist now fidgeted with as he regarded the piano thoughtfully.

The ball hadn't moved the piano at all, not even an inch. Neither had the hot westerly breeze bringing in the afternoon dust. It didn't appear to be hanging in the sky, just stuck. It had the weight and presence of any normal piano, but it was in the wrong place.

The crowd gathered, and discussed their theories. People took selfies with the 'Ghost Piano', the 'Sky Steinway'. The town cop put some witches hats in a rough circle under it and told everyone to keep their distance, in case whatever was holding it up ... stopped. Within an hour the publican had named a cocktail after it, and was promoting it on the hotel Facebook page. Soon after, it had its own Twitter account. A girl posted video to TikTok, shouting, 'Go home piano, you're drunk!'

Somehow, nobody saw the piano disappear, either. There was a noise like high-voltage electricity, a crack like a stock-whip, and when everyone looked up it was gone. It hadn't fallen, caught fire or flown away – it simply wasn't there any more. Some people claimed there was a strange lingering odour, but others said they couldn't smell anything. A week later people were still talking about it; a month later, not so much. The Twitter account went dormant, its final tweet: 'Float like a piano, sting like a bee.'

In a locked drawer at the town pharmacy was a small broken piece of timber moulding.

After the Calm

by Anna Russell

AFTER TWO DAYS of constant wind and heavy cloud, two days of lectures and training and jumping out of earthbound planes, Ruby was ready to quit; but on the Sunday morning the sky cleared, and it was on.

She was scheduled for the second run, with Gryff and Jamie. Kevin, that scarred old veteran, was their instructor. Ruby was to go first and as she knelt on the floor of the plane, knee-to-knee with Kevin beside the open doorway, she felt quite calm. She'd had the training.

'Now remember, the plane'll stop and you'll step out onto the wing-strut, look at me, I'll shout one two three, and you'll throw yourself back like a starfish, belly button to the sky, and the chute will open. Keep your legs straight until the chute opens, Okay? Enjoy yourself.'

Ruby climbed onto the strut and looked back at Kevin. He yelled one, two, three, and she didn't move, couldn't move, she was frozen to the wing. 'Come on Ruby, one, two, three, go, now.'

Still she couldn't move, then her foot slipped and she was gone. All memory of the starfish gone, her legs bent and she spun, screaming 'shiiitttt' as she went down. Then the chute opened and everything was suddenly still and silent.

Time stops when you're parachuting, until the last few metres. Ruby hadn't even looked for the landing spot before she went into a tree. The chute caught on a branch and she almost hit the trunk, having enough presence of mind to push off it with her foot, before swinging to a stop two metres above the ground. That's not gonna kill me, she thought, releasing the canopy and dropping to the ground. As she did, she heard a low moan and dangling in mid-air her eyes saw a pair of legs.

'Participle,' she called, 'is that you?'

Nights in a Brothel

Saturday Morning

by Chris McIntosh

'MY GOD, IT'S like a brothel in here!' shouts my mum as she barges in, dragging the vacuum cleaner behind her. I groan loudly and pull the covers up over my head, knowing she'll head straight for the window to let in the unwelcome sun. I clench my eyes shut, pretending that none of this is happening but powerless to stop it.

'When were you last in a brothel?' I grumble. She ignores me of course, flinging open the curtains then skilfully tip-toeing back across my mess-strewn floor.

'Ten minutes,' she says as she disappears down the hall. She says it brightly, but we both know it's a threat.

I could doze here for another hour at least, but I know her ten minutes is really five. She'll come bouncing back in and that whining bloody machine will be the end of me. Besides, I don't want her touching my stuff. Forcing myself up, I sit on the edge of my bed yawning and look around the room. I can't imagine any brothel looking like this disaster area.

Can't be bothered standing, so I kneel on the floor and start sorting clothes into piles – clean, worn, and needing a wash. One T-shirt smells so bad I give it its own pile. Rubbish into the bin.

Homework and textbooks onto the already crowded desk. Quick check under the bed for soiled tissues. Oh, there's that other charging cable.

That reminds me to do a quick digital clean-up too, and I wake up my laptop. Close the cam-girl websites. Pay a tip to Crystal on OnlyFans, before closing that too. Who even needs to spend a night in a brothel these days, when you can practically bring the brothel to you?

Browsing history cleared; battery on charge; room now safe enough to let Mum intrude. I head to the kitchen for breakfast.

Watching

by Barbara Maxwell

THE LOUNGE ROOM picture window afforded Vera an excellent view of the street. Rene often wondered if her friend had chosen the house for this very reason as she knew all the comings and goings in the neighbourhood and enjoyed immensely being 'in the know'.

Today, as they sipped their tea, Vera was consumed with curiosity about exactly what was happening at number 46, directly across the road. Ted had put the house on the market within three months of Colleen's death and Vera was reporting on all that she had seen and heard.

'I don't know Rene, I'm frankly shocked and appalled, what on earth would Colleen say if she was alive?'

'Vera, I don't think we should assume that is what is happening, although it seems so unlike Ted, he has always been such a respectable sort of man. Why, he was on the P and F with my Fred, bless his soul, and worked so hard for the school.'

'That is beside the point Rene, it is what he's doing now! Colleen worked so hard for all those years doing night shifts at the hospital. But it is true, why, John Blythe was dropping off a customer across the road, and Rene, there was Ted, bold as brass, walking in.'

'Maybe he is lonely and just looking for company Vera.'

Vera huffed, 'Well the moving van is leaving now, I guess they'll be back tomorrow but it is so strange.'

Just then, a car pulled up and Vera peered hard, exclaiming 'Why, it's John Toohey, our solicitor.'

Across the road, Ted walked out to meet John, 'I've got all the documents here Ted, I just need you to sign them and Colleen's business will be sold.'

John chuckled as he surveyed the street, 'I bet Vera is up there watching as always, but she'll never know Colleen was no nurse. Well, let's go inside so I can sign those papers for the sale of the brothel.'

Vera was none the wiser.

Grata Iuvenis

by Anna Russell

THE TOUR STARTED badly with the bus an hour late collecting Adrian from Izmir, allowing only twenty minutes at the House of the Virgin Mary, fifteen minutes too long as far as Adrian was concerned. He'd glanced in the chapel, seen all the selfie-takers, and chosen the terrace and a glass of tea.

Then it was the silk factory, tragic, the leather coat atelier, a rip-off, and a mediocre lunch of mezze and wine in the garden under a tree.

They reached Ephesus with one hour to closing and Murtaza, the guide, dragged them along at a ridiculous pace until Adrian gave up, tucking himself on a warm stone seat in the lavatorium, his face to the sun. He must have fallen asleep for next he knew the giggling tourists had gone and it was getting dark.

Adrian hurried to the entrance to see the last car driving off. He tried phoning the tourist agency, but it rang out, ripped his sleeve while attempting to climb the gate, gave up. Feeling exposed, he found an enclosed space at the brothel, a foot, heart, woman, and money purse carved into the stone lintel. He ate a sesame bar, drank water, and looked at Instagram before turning off his phone.

Then he heard a mellifluous voice saying, '*Grata iuvenis pro quibus voluptatibus tibi offerre possumus,*' which somehow he knew meant 'Welcome youth, to all the pleasures we offer'.

He woke to something soft and warm on his leg, and opening his eyes saw a large marmalade cat which maintained eye contact while needling Adrian's thigh. Hearing voices he pushed the cat off and rose stiffly to his feet, before rushing to the doorway. Outside was his tour group.

'Ah, Adrian bey,' said Murtaza, with a smirk, '*Nazilsin*. I see you have already found the house of pleasures.' Then he proceeded with the tour.

The Bands Played On

by D'Arcy Lloyd

LOU APPEARED, PLEADING for Holly who'd plucked her eyebrows and shaved her legs. She soon arrived from behind, whispered, 'Hey babe, take a walk on the wild side? Let's go doo do doo.'

Taupin arrived in Elton's iridescent balls. He ordered the sweet painted lady who likes getting paid for being laid. Right place then!

Eric landed like an Animal, declared we're in the House of Rising Sun, uncertain whether nights in brothels are the ruin of men women or both.

Freddie exploded onto the scene and roared, 'She's a killer queen, gunpowder, gelatine, dynamite with a laser beam. Gotta try!'

Then Mick with hips 'n' lips sidled in, insisted on meeting the Memphis gin-soaked honky-tonk bar-room queen.

Fogarty groaned. He was wailing as he went off back to some Cajun Queen in the bayou. Could still be heard as he thundered through the rains in Virginia.

When Gordon squeezed in howling Roxanne didn't have to sell her body to the night, The Police stung and silenced him.

The bar-room couldn't have hummed any harder, until Brooker, looking a whiter shade of excess, skipped the light fandango cooing for sixteen vestal virgins.

The brothel's bar was chockers when Kinky Davies popped in pleading for Lola from old Soho, who looks like a woman and talks like a man!

La Belle rolled her eyes, took pity, and suggested a Moody Blues night in white satin, winked and said, 'He'll be home for 9 to 5 in a grey flannel life … but not eating Marmalade.'

Dean and Sammy returned from the dead and crooned legato, 'everybody loves somebody sometime.' Twenty sets of eyebrows rose doubtfully.

The old virgin spinster woke and whined to no one who was there, 'That was an impossible dream, for it was definitely not my way.'

Wild Days in Dakota

by Narelle Fernance

THE CONVERSATION HAD lulled. Sam appeared to be staring into the bottom of his coffee cup, uncertain how to proceed.

'Is something troubling you?' asked Fred, concerned that his friend had suddenly felt he was in uncharted waters.

'Well, yes ... and no,' stuttered Sam, glancing up and then quickly finding interest in the cup again.

Fred waited.

'I haven't talked much about my younger days in America, before I came north to Ottawa. Now I am here to ask for your support of my application for membership of the Turf Club committee, I don't know that this is a good time to start. But you have taken me into your confidence, revealing that you, too, have in another life travelled outside the law. Then again, I know that you were forced into that line of business by the legislators, who made it impossible for you to live lawfully. Alas, I can't claim that explanation!'

'You intrigue me.'

'Yes, well, I had to leave Missouri in a hurry due to some events in a dark alley in which I had been involved, and I thought I should head west on the Oregon Trail. Another wagon's passengers were "working girls". They were headed for Deadwood and the Black Hills of Dakota where rich gold deposits had been discovered in 1874, the previous year.'

'Oh, I see.'

'Well, they seemed like a lively bunch. I took a particular shine to Michelle, a Frenchie, who purred rather than spoke, and enjoyed many nights in the brothel, hanging around the saloon most days. One thing led to another, some cowpoke with too much moolah and whisky, also took a shine to Michelle. I pulled my Colt, and he fell backwards over a table. I absconded for the North West Territory.'

'Ah, I understand your hesitancy in revealing that side of your past,' Fred nodded solemnly.

That Might Not Be Enough

Devotion

by Barbara Maxwell

MEG AND EMMA stood in front of the house looking at the recently neglected garden, overgrown so quickly in the steamy Brisbane summer. Their beloved Mother had happily laboured there right to the end and now a skip dominated the house and garden.

The two women put their arms around each other and entered the house, neither relishing the task ahead. Inside, the house transported them back many years as Meg gently ran her fingers over the hall furniture, familiar but somehow different. Both Meg and Emma felt the loss of the energy that had always existed through the presence of their mother.

They worked quietly and efficiently, sorting clothes and odds and ends, a pile for Vinnies, one for Meg and one for Emma. A few requested items were to go to their mother's friends. The days passed, they moved from room to room, reminiscing as they went. Photo albums, books, childhood belongings that had been cherished but long forgotten. Their mother's knitting, a partially completed jumper for one of the grandchildren lay on the table beside her chair. At night, Meg and Emma sipped wine and recalled their childhood, joyous and loving with their ever busy mother showering their father and her girls with love.

They'd saved the sewing room till last; it would be the hardest, their mother's domain. Busy always with a project underway. There was the sewing machine and sure enough, a partially completed dress was scattered around. The cupboards they knew would be packed with fabrics. Remember, they said as they opened the doors, we'd shop for the material for our dresses each season, the patterns would say two yards or two and a half, but mum would always say that might not be enough. They laughed at the memory but there on the shelves were two exquisite quilts, each marked with their names, each square a piece of fabric from the dresses of their lives, lovingly crafted into a gift of memories.

Maslow's Hierarchy

by D'Arcy Lloyd

BILL'S TOLD HIS fencing crew to pack up, job's done! I like Bill, and he's fond of me – we're a right royal mutual-admiration couple.

Nearly time to say cheerio. Wanna say good riddance to his new Second. He's fond of mocking my humans, reckons getting their best friend the chop or a shock collar is the way to go – dream on, sadist! He can't fathom spending thousands on raising the perimeter's fence for a 'damned dog'. Grr … he'll be damned!

The crew is shifting their gear out to the street. Time to come out of hiding.

Bill's greeting me, 'G'day Maslow. Where've you been boy?' Bill can scratch behind my ears forever.

Second's spotted me. 'So, this is the famous Maslow! Handsome bugger, but there's no bloody way he can jump that fence!'

For a second there … I was warming to him, barring the bugger bit. As for his reckoning? Once they're out the gate, he is on!

Ah, here comes Alison, my number one human. Bill is busy telling Second, 'He can jump, and he can climb!'

'Nah! That's a myth,' says Second.

Alison's joining in. 'Oh no, the security cameras caught him in the act.'

Uh oh! She's looking at me with that radar look.

'In fact, that ridiculous new height still might not be enough. All done? Cheerio men.'

Yep, she's clocked me, so I'll follow her back to the house, good boy that I am. I'll give the crew three minutes lead.

Alison's on our gate's videocam. 'Forget something, Bill?'

'Missin' somethin' Alison?'

The Big Bugger's moving into Alison's view, my twenty-five kilos skirting his bulbous neck. I was gonna bite 'im, but now? Now he's scratching behind my ears – mmm!

They'll be back soon enough.

The Gift of Giving

by Kris Nissam

THE GIFT OF giving and sharing in realms other than money is a complex but awesome trade table. A smile can be worth more than ever imagined to a stranger or someone walking the same path as yourself.

In many fraught, dangerous or shared occasions, as simple as shopping at a market for food, a smile gives warmth to the whole situation.

Spending time in the Royal Children's Hospital with children and grandchildren the immeasurable pain, grief, concern and absolute fear of losing them could all be relieved by a smile from a stranger suffering the same situation. The smile turns to a hug and shared tears when they lost their child.

The dusty dry paddocks and then the flood creeping ever closer to the homestead tests one's endurance to the limit, and as you feel your last bit of strength about to dissolve, a smile from a farmer relieves the shared pain.

So, taking on the self care, so often advised, I booked in for a massage after rolling the ute. That was a relief that no amount of money could pay for. Not only that, the woman requested to paint a portrait of myself and the Brahmans.

I was deeply honoured and a little embarrassed. After many sketches, photos and months of work the day came when the painting was unveiled. Unbelievably beautiful and accurate on a rounded canvas and the colours: superb. The essence of the art was a window into my world.

So, the question was asked, 'How much do I owe you?' and the paltry sum for the paint was mentioned. 'That might not be enough!' I exclaimed in disbelief.

Quietly, I went back into the massage room and deposited a significant sum of money into the crystal bowl on the altar. I also left many blessings and wishes for good health and great fortune for this amazing person.

Random

by Anna Russell

HOW DID YOU leave?

How?

Yes, not why, we all know why. How did you decide that it was the right time, that it was safe?

Oh, it's kind of a weird story, serendipitous, or maybe random, I don't know. You remember when I went to WA for that conference? Well, I was skiving off some sessions as usual, wandering around Fremantle, and when I was walking through a kind of arcade with lots of different shops, at the end there was a sign advertising a clairvoyant. Her door was open and I went in.

She was sitting behind a white table, which was completely bare except for a notepad and pencil, maybe it was a pen, I don't know. The woman told me to close the door and sit down, then she asked, 'What is your question?'

It was all a bit abrupt, no preliminaries, I hadn't had a chance to prepare, and I just said, 'My partner.'

'His name?' she asked.

I said, 'David' and she wrote the name in the middle of the sheet of paper, in pencil or in pen, and placed her hand over it with her eyes closed.

'You must leave him,' she said, 'he's making you very ill.'

'Ill?' I asked.

'The anxiety, the stress and fear, the black energy. I know that you're afraid to leave, but you should be more afraid to stay.'

'But he—' I started to say, and she interrupted me.

'He threatens suicide, I know. But I can't see him doing it, and if he does, it will not be your fault. You have to look after yourself. I see that you doubt me but did you not come here so I would tell you to leave. Have I not given you reason?'

'But that might not be enough,' I said.

'How many reasons have you to stay?' she asked, and I came home and left him.

Beginnings of Possibilities

by Narelle Fernance

FRED COULD HEAR Francesca humming to herself in the kitchen and took a moment to stand at the window looking to the west. The lace curtains were barely moving in the warm Canadian breeze as the last rays of the sun shone in streaks to the clouds, reflecting yellow and pink haze.

As he gazed, he became aware how relaxed he felt, and began to think he was looking at an Australian scene. His Mary Ann rode into the clearing on her favourite mare, a bay with three white stockings. Mary Ann was dressed in that familiar riding garb she preferred when they had ridden the ranges together. She looked at him steadily, then smiled and saluted. With a delighted whoop and a flourish, she swung the mare, down past the granite rocks and gum trees, towards the singing brook under the willow branches.

He stood a moment longer, experiencing the familiar longing, but now also peace. Mary Ann had given her blessings, that he should move on. He had never felt comfortable with that thought before, but now everything was in order. He knew that he should see where life led. When he turned from the window he realised that Francesca was standing in the doorway. She was holding a heavy serving tray, complete with silver cover. She seemed uncertain, until he grinned and strode towards her, relieving her of her burden.

The tray was given pride of place, the lid removed. The aroma of wondrous cuisine was pure pleasure. There was baked pheasant, pork and quail, surrounded by garden vegetables, all browned to perfection.

With a grin, he indicated for Francesca to sit, sliding her chair into position. 'Well,' he said, 'this calls for a nice bottle of Chateau Clair, I think.'

'That might not be enough,' she replied. On realisation of her boldness, her cheeks burned, but she smiled, as their eyes met.

The Price is High

by Chris McIntosh

WHEN I WALK in he's already there, sitting at the table in the corner with a mountain of burgers and fries in front of him. He doesn't say anything as I approach, just smiles with his perfect white teeth and gestures to the pile, knowing I'll be hungry.

We eat in silence, and he barely takes his eyes off me. I keep mine on the food. When I'm finished I start fidgeting, so I sit on my hands. He waits for me to ask for it. He always makes me ask. He sits there with his bulging muscles, tight white T-shirt and nine-hundred-dollar watch, and makes me beg.

'Have you got it?' I almost whisper.

'Of course.'

I reach across the table and we pretend to hold hands briefly. He doesn't even count it. He knows I'll be short – again.

'That ... might not be enough.' His eyes start to wander. I've worn a baggy jumper to try and hide in, but it doesn't stop him. Under the table, his leg brushes against mine. I feel disgusting.

'Please. I can pay more next time.'

'You've said that before.' He casually chews on a leftover fry. 'You've said a lot of things before, made a lot of promises. You know I can take this somewhere else if you don't want it.' He moves a napkin and there's a zip-lock bag underneath, grains like rock salt glinting in the sun. It's been sitting there the whole time, right on the table. I realise I've stopped breathing. 'You owe me, and if you want this, you know what you need to do. Otherwise, I can just walk out right now.'

I lower my head. Every time he's asked, I've said no; but I knew it would come to this. I nod slowly.

'Cool!' he says cheerfully, standing to leave and pocketing the bag. 'Come for a drive with me. I know somewhere quiet.'

Peeing

Bonding Over Chaucer
by D'Arcy Lloyd

GRAND-AUNT AGGY WAS known as *the last Edwardian child* for being born the minute King Edward VII died. She was later known as *the Bolter* … both perfect.

Five husbands, all staggeringly wealthy. At one-hundred and two she remained fit, sharp, widowed, loaded. She beguilingly held her own on any topic, but on etiquette, grammar and style she was superlative.

At her sumptuous penultimate family gathering, Philip – my cousin several times removed – arrived late and stunned the packed room. We'd not met before, though I'd been forewarned to brace for oozing drop-dead privilege – influential networks, global lifestyle, entitled, kit-and-caboodle! – until his incongruous Aussie twang split my ears!

'G'day everyone. Pissing down out there! An' I need the WC to pee.'

The room gasped. Buttocks clenched!

Aggy roared at the base of her contralto, 'Philip! You will refrain from vulgar language.'

He froze! Frowned? *Then* … with twinkling eyes, smugly tapped

The Canterbury Tales on her lap.

'Which language would that be Aggy? Reckon it should be Chaucer's? I hear your Number Five, Aggy, was rather fond of reciting, "The Wives of Bath".'

He winked at the room and exited in twanging full throated recitation:

'Nothing escaped him of the pain and woe

That Socrates had with his spouses two

How Xanthippe threw *piss* upon his head

This hapless man sat still, as he were dead

He wiped his head, no more durst he complain

Then ere –'

Philip's head shot back around the door.

'– the thunder ceases, comes the rain.'

Aggy was joyful! 'Well done my boy! Vulgar Latin or not, *listen* to how pissing conquers priggy po-faced peeing. Can you recite it as writ? Yes, of course you can.'

In moments, their mutual admiration was born. In moments more, Aggy breathed, winked, smiled, died.

Jarinda Force of Fire

by Brydie O'Shea

KHAN LIFTED HIS head from his dog blanket, but only just. The left side of his face was the size of a cricket ball. It distorted Khan's head. I saw he was peeing. He looked at me, apologetic for causing concern.

'My poor Boy,' I said. Khan licked my hand, picking up on my Something-Not-Right vibe.

I made the call. Then drove Khan to the vet.

The vet said, 'Khan is the oldest German Shepherd I've ever seen. He's only lasted this long because of your good care. I doubt he'll last an operation. It will just prolong his pain.'

The vet looked uncomfortable, until he went for the kill.

'I think it's best to euthanise,' he said.

They spoke of The Green Dream, but I for one never trusted dreams and I wrapped my body around Khan in a Locked-Jawed-One-Last-Hug, while they shaved his leg.

He cried; a plaintive, frightened whimper, like an unweaned puppy. That was hard.

'I love you Khan. Know Darling Khan, how much I always loved you.'

He withdrew his paw. His eyes pleaded. He was my wolf cub; my shadow, but still I let them hold his foreleg tight, to administer the needle.

Khan was the sick one, but my throat was explosive. I felt the pain. It was real; it stabbed my chest, sliced my heart, and sunk in my core. Both of us laboured to breathe.

I held him, my face buried in fur. Khan was never one to be held, but this time I needed to hold him. Did not want to let him go.

Then I lost sight of him through my tears (was he swimming in the Woronora?)

But I was with him when the flame in Khan's eyes died and the light extinguished in Jarinda Force of Fire.

An Abandoned Chase

by Narelle Fernance

THUNDERBOLT SLOUCHED AT his ease in the saddle. One leg drawn up resting across Combo's shoulder. His apprentice was not so relaxed, casting anxious glances up the road. But the band played on. Not only had the bushranger stolen twenty pounds from Worth's Band, but had convinced them to play a march for his trouble.

It was 1868, just north of Tenterfield. Thunderbolt and Will had won a tidy sum from the bookies at the races where the band had been playing. But not satisfied, Thunderbolt knew that the winning horse, Minstrel, would be ridden home along there. The plan was to relieve the owner of some of the prize-money. But the German band had happened along first.

Having been entertained by the Germans, Thunderbolt saluted and wheeled Combo at full gallop, headed across-country to his hideout of granite boulders. He drew rein at the top of the ridge, with Will close behind him. Alas, not all was as they would wish. Three reasonable-looking saddled horses were tethered near the entrance. The bushranger noticed that the riders were in civvies, he none-the-less had little doubt they were police.

Worse, one had seen him! The bushrangers swung their mounts to the south, heading straight towards a cliff-like rock face, the Traps now in hot pursuit. When Thunderbolt got to a thicket of myall, he directed Will to turn off to the right, knowing himself to be the main quarry. A wide chasm in the rock lay ahead. Gripping Combo hard, he leant forward. Rider and thoroughbred sailed across the fifteen feet drop, and upwards into the hills.

Turning back from the top and looking down at the riders below, halted at the chasm, Thunderbolt coo-eed to them when he noted that they had given up. One had dismounted and was peeing on a nearby stump. Raising his hat in salute, Thunderbolt swung his horse to disappear between the boulders.

Running the Gauntlet

by Anna Russell

I TRIED NOT to cry when mum left. She'd said, 'Don't cry pet, I'll be back in the morning before you go to theatre,' but I was afraid in that horrible ward. I'd been in hospital before, lots of times, but not such a big old one as this with so many old ladies. When mum took me to the toilet I'd counted fifteen beds on one side and fifteen on the other which added up to thirty. Plus me, but they were making me sleep in a cot. I hadn't slept in a cot since I was three and I was too old for it then. And they all looked at me, especially the little old lady in the bed next to me, she'd been staring all day. But in a kind way, not a scary way.

It was getting dark when mum left and the lights were turned on but that just made it worse. I could see but not see. I hadn't had anything to drink for hours however much they told me I should, but I still needed to wee. I always needed to wee. I knew I had to go to the toilet or I'd wet the bed and get into trouble. I climbed out of the cot and put on my dressing gown and slippers and walked down the aisle between the old ladies. They were calling me and holding out their hands. One tried to give me lollies and told me my hair was pretty, and another one asked why I was there. I said that I wasn't allowed to eat and that I had a Golden Staph and then I ran as fast as I could and a nurse caught me and took me to the toilet just in time. And when I came out she washed my hands for me and dried between each finger, very softly, and took me back to bed.

Communities

Memories

by Barbara Maxwell

IT WAS SATURDAY and I was folding Mum's laundry ready to take. Anxiety and sadness mingled as I thought of the visit. What would be her mood, would she know me today or simply be angry like last weekend when she'd accused me of taking her away from her home?

Each week I'd tried to find something to do, read a story, do a crossword with her. The poetry reading had been successful for a few visits. Mum's eyes had lit up as she recalled the words of Wordsworth, Tennyson and others, but now she remained dull and listless when I read it to her. I had a new plan today. Sorting through Mum's house, I'd found her old photos in a shoebox. They were unmarked and as I navigated the long drive, I thought perhaps she would recall the people and places in the photos.

Arriving, I greeted Mum with a peck on the cheek and set to work putting her clothes away and dusting and tidying the room all the while chatting and filling Mum in on all the family news. Today Mum was passive, inert, disinterested. I sat beside her and pulled out the old photos, could she tell me about them, who the people were?

Her eyes remained glazed over as I showed her the photos from her nursing days. Then came the photos of Mum with her sister Mary, dressed up and standing with their father. She brightened, her body moved and straightened as she took the pictures, we were going to a dance she said, at Coraki. Father would drive us, we'd spend all afternoon getting ready, every Saturday night in the season, she laughed. The community halls would be crowded, and Father would wait outside in the car or around the back with the men and the beer keg. On she talked, eyes bright, years seem to fade away. I sat and listened, watching my mother reappear for this one afternoon, rejoicing in her young life, dancing from one hall to another.

The Other

by Anna Russell

HER FAVOURITE PLACE when she was feeling scared or upset or just needing to be alone was a reverse mound, a divot, a shape created on the slope where a tree had been wrenched from the earth by its roots. A crater in fact, made by man.

There were many of these but this one was perfect for her small form, deep enough for her to be hidden from view, long enough to stretch out, easy to clamber out of when her father called her.

The problem was that it wasn't on their land, it belonged to the others and was just across the border, hence it was surrounded by long grass and 'weeds', which infuriated her father because the 'weeds' were undisciplined and didn't know their place. Because of the long grass, the 'weeds', the re-colonisation, or rather the homecoming of native trees and bushes, the house of the others was hidden from view even though it was high on the hill directly opposite their house, which rose from the earth as if burst from it and was surrounded by nothing but foxgloves, oleander and larkspur, her mother's favourite. And groomed green grass with its strain kept pure from the stain of native grasses by the use of targeted poisons.

Her father was sure that the others were looking at him, at them, and had taken to sitting out the back in the evenings with his beer, even though it meant being seared by the setting summer sun. And it meant missing out on the view of the ocean with its sunset glittering beyond the house of the others.

She didn't know what the others thought about all of this, though she sometimes sat beside one of them on the school bus. They didn't talk about their home, their community.

Emerald Hill

by Kris Nissam

I'm heading out to Emerald Hill
For a music concert, what a thrill
An enormous harp accompanied by a guitar
All of us have travelled far

The tiny town with a small outback hall
The concert keenly anticipated by all
The rumble outside of the passing trains
Tractors working the wide-open plains

The little boy playing quietly in the dirt
While mum carries the baby and hitches her skirt
A warm welcome extended to all
By the CWA and food galore

A tiny town with not even a store
But streamers and palm leaves decorate the hall
The whole community working side by side
A comment whispered might have been snide

But there we were with musicians renowned
Visiting this tiny unknown town
They said that they loved the interactions with the people
Rather than being up on stage like a steeple
Being able to interact with one and all
Outback in the Emerald Hill Hall

Some of the men were unable to attend
Irrigating and driving on the farming hell bent
The wind and the weather wait for no-one
Oh, watch out here comes that bloody sun

From the babies sleeping in their prams
To all the dear old Pops and Grans
And everyone in between
All went to create this community scene

To those unseen such as the gardeners, painters and cleaners

And the crew that displayed the bright colourful streamers

Thank you for the insights into your community

Sharing your stories and doing your duty

The crew from Sydney also travelling, organising and performing

They must have got up real early this morning

An awesome performance with worldwide reputation

Right beside this railway station

Only four such duos in all the world

As around us their music crescendoed and swirled

Thank you to all who participated

In this community recitation

Silent Footfalls

by D'Arcy Lloyd

'Let 'em go, they're useless.'

'Let them go!'

'Yeah, who cares?'

'Who cares!'

THROUGH HIGHS AND lows, Waterloo Station's three best buildings have survived for over 120 years. John Sinclair's 1926 journal confirms that twelve additional buildings existed amongst Waterloo Station's community. A mud map accompanied the list, but it and those buildings are missing now.

Does the whereabouts anywhere of once-buildings matter, whether grand or utilitarian? They are simply inanimate bits tacked, whacked or even masterfully woven together for shelter, a tad of comfort, through to grandly extravagant.

Inextricably linked with all communities – from family to global – is the creation of place where safety and security and an aspirational prism of trust and belonging are sought. Some find it, many die searching for it, or hoping it will come … tomorrow.

Tribal communities formed to survive. Today's gargantuan global population drives an anxiety-fuelled belief that if not a member of its community, an individual is a misfit, not worthy. Regardless of classification: place, interest, identity, need, or practice, each implies a dependence on some form of built environment: castle, stadium, hut, lean-to.

What does it mean to let a place die or be wilfully destroyed? What does it do to the spirit of place and communities from ancient bora to balls whose traces become silent footfalls?

Close to dereliction in 2001, Waterloo Station's current owners have since brought bold commitment to restoring and conserving its built and cultural heritage. Neither individuals nor families would have ever communed on Waterloo without the spirit of natural and built environments. They fuelled enterprise, stock, precious clips, annual charity Woolshed balls, celebrations; simply, communities.

Once disused buildings decay, many unconscionably subscribe to the demolisher's model of 'knock 'em down', then dumbly opine about the relentless collapse of communities.

The Witch's Tree

by Brydie O'Shea

I WAS ONCE a seed of the Never-Never and I danced on a summer, scorched breeze. My thrill of dispersal was powerful but short-winded – within seconds I careered from the sky, impacted the earth, ate dirt and took root. For all the pain of my journey, I had travelled no long distance. Then it became apparent I had not escaped. I was in a grove, well within the remnant clutches of my mother The Widow Maker. At least I did not fall victim to her toxic chemicals. I landed far enough from her to be deemed uncompetitive. I fell into mud above the swirling waterline of the river 'they' called The Honey.

Honey? Does that not sound enchanting? But do not be deceived. Do not overlook how closely allied honey is to the sting.

I didn't take to my habitat cordially; dominated by ancient gums, grown grim and bent with time. Their warped branches itched to stunt my growth, and I spent my youth in the shadow of eucalypts, manacled to the river's edge.

I fought long battles trying to renege my origins, but I didn't win. Eventually my roots, like all the parent trees, crawled into the river traipsing like funnel-webs' legs making haunts for Murray Cod.

At the start, The Honey was like royal jelly. By the time I grew old, it was vinegar.

And I could not help but conform, to everything dry sclerophyll. The sun increased my cambium, and I grew. Bending. Leaning ever toward my mother. I abhorred the thought of being like Her. But there lay the irony. I may have been propagated from her cutting instead of sown from her seed, for I was like a clone. I couldn't fight nature. And in the end, I inherited her heartwood.

It was rotten.

The Ottawa Turf Club of 1895

by Narelle Fernance

FRED WAS BECOMING uneasy as he sat yarning to Sam. He kept reminding himself that he should have been enjoying the occasion. Sitting on the patio, he had been taking pleasure in the company of a neighbour, with whom he had grown an affinity in recent years. The fact that today's exchanges had disclosed that they both had a bit of a shabby past was bonding, rather than something that might cause uneasiness.

He dismissed his agitation, shrugging off rising negativity. Anyway, it would be lunchtime, and Francesca would have the table set in his study. They planned to work on a submission to the Turf Club, supporting Sam's application for committee membership.

'So my friend, if you are starting to get a little famished we can relocate to my study. Francesca will have the luncheon table ready, I'm sure. Then, we will get on with filling in the necessary paperwork for your submission.'

'I feel very humbled that you are going to all this trouble for me, Fred,' began Sam, as he stood up. He pushed the easy chair forward, to lean on the back. 'I think the committee has been doing a good job. Certainly to the standard of any turf club being run by other local communities. But could it be time to up the ante, and make the Ottawa Turf Club just that little bit better than the rest. New ideas, thus a new appeal to racegoers would attract a different group of horse lovers. That in turn, will attract new spectators, meaning more money in the club coffers.'

'Yes indeed,' agreed Fred, leading the way indoors towards his study. But as he pondered his irritation, he knew he was not as excited for his companion as he should have been.

Food, Friend or Foe?

by Chris McIntosh

FORWARD. FORWARD. LEFT. Forward. Right. Stop.

What is this? Something is in the way.

Food? No. Friend? No. Foe? No.

It is in the way. Move it.

The ant grabs, and tries to lift, but the thing is too heavy. The ant knows it can lift big things, but this is too big for one ant. It bites down hard, and manages to peel away a tiny triangle of bark from the side of the twig. Hmmm, now what to do with it? If it was food, the ant would take the bark back to the nest and feed it to the compost heap. This bark doesn't compost very well though, and this species of ant doesn't use it for building, so it has no use. Off to the side of the track somewhere.

A friend approaches.

'Something is in the way. Help me move it.'

'Is it food?'

'No.'

The friend tries to lift the thing, and discovers it is too big. Friend takes a bite.

As each friend approaches, they are asked to help, and they do so without complaint. Some don't need to be asked – they see the situation and immediately volunteer. Others head back towards the nest to recruit more friends. Soon there are many, each making a small contribution to the task. They are much stronger together. The last parts of the twig are small enough to be dragged or carried away, and now the path is clear. The ants mingle for a while, some checking that there is nothing else that needs moving, others making sure there really is no food.

The first ant has forgotten what it was doing before it came across the obstacle, but here is a nice clear path for it to follow.

'Thank you for helping, friends. Goodbye.'

Forward. Forward. Right. Forward …

Memoir

The Birds

by Anna Russell

WE WERE TOLD to approach red-headed Michael, a fisherman at Malin Harbour who owned a boat called the *Kittiwake*, and when we asked him if he'd take us to the island he said, 'Surely I will.' By three in the afternoon we were standing on a little jetty on Inishtrahull, as Michael sailed off with his escort of seals. The island didn't take long to explore, just a short walk between the defunct lighthouse and the automated one, the abandoned stone village, hundreds of red deer and thousands of rabbits in between.

At ten p.m. I was sitting on my mat outside the tent experiencing a golden hour, that lasted six. From time to time I would look up to count rabbits, always stopping at fifty, for what was the point of counting further?

Waking early next morning I left the others sleeping and went to bathe in a private little cove I'd spotted the day before. It was deep and perfectly circular, its entrance to the sea obscured by a wall of rock. I walked carefully down a narrow path which spiralled round the cliff like the inside of a nautilus shell, all to the applause, or condemnation, of thousands of nesting seabirds, singing the songs of their people.

At the bottom, no sand, just stones in diminishing sizes and in a range of colours from blood to green, interspersed with a flotsam and jetsam of driftwood sculptures and sea glass, blue, why always blue? Is Bombay Sapphire so ubiquitous?

As I entered the water and lay down carefully on my stony bed, I looked up, twenty metres up and saw more clearly my loud and raucous audience, their screams and screeches echoing off the natural amphitheatre, and I felt smaller and more insignificant than the smallest petrel. And I was filled with exhilaration, and terror.

A Trail of Description

by Kris Nissam

SO, WHO ARE you? 'I have 27 capes,' is my standard reply.

1. Me myself and I. Physically, mentally, emotionally and spiritually
2. Daughter
3. Mother of those dead and alive
4. Family member with all its nuances
5. Animal lover and protector
6. Conservationist, saving remote bushland areas
7. Horse lover, owner, educator and friend
8. Owner builder
9. Surfer girl
10. Motorbike rider
11. Photographer for fun, transformed into exhibiting artist
12. Great cook. Creative at times, resourceful when needed
13. Wife of many, we all had lessons to learn

14. Guitar, harp, ocarina and piano player

15. Teacher, tutor, mentor and principal.

16. Labyrinth creator and facilitator

17. Alternative health practitioner

18. Wholistic Counsellor

19. Friend to many

20. Mate to the special few

21. Reader, writer, poet, author

22. Able to see the humour in all situations

23. Organisational whiz kid

24. Farmer in a natural but sensible way

25. Optimist to the extreme

26. Taurean, stubborn, independent and protector of others

27. Blonde, youthful … now grey and gracefully aging

That's who I am!

Malignant Encounters

by D'Arcy Lloyd

One

WEEK THREE, TERM one, 1973. The Principal welcomed me back from a gap year. This was my last shot at vanquishing an ambivalence towards teaching's methods that had long stymied my hunger to learn. Principal encouraged me bravely to aim higher. I declined. He conceded. Next, sign-in with department heads.

First stop, English. Tall, '70's look-at-me blonde mo, arrived in '72. Shorts and long socks, really! He led me halfway down a corridor – odd I thought – leant on a door jamb, crossed a leg over the shin of the other, odder still. His actions seemed … casually deliberate.

'I'm not qualified to teach first-level English, but …'

Who confesses that to a student! He did *and* re-confirmed his reckless confidence, then oscillated between tones of fellowship and spite; and tossing coins around in his groin pocket. That bizarre scene returns unbidden, vividly.

'First level is already in place. *You're* late back. I'm not taking any second leveller out of 6E1. Go to 6E2. *Just* come to first level extras.'

Acutely aware I'd been marginalised; I was formulating a protest when he un-propped himself and spread his legs, ominously. Each word was cutthroat – inexplicable – demoralising.

'*Nobody* wants you here, Miss Lloyd. The students *don't* want you here. The teachers don't want *you* here.'

Though ludicrous, I was stunned, baffled, shattered. Rendered speechless to protest, my distrust was cast.

'Now let's talk about what you will do. Remember Laura and Nick (peers repeating)? They are brilliant, *brilliant!* We're doing poetry appreciation. You know what that is, don't you? Paul McCartney – one has Eleanor Rigby, the other Penny Lane. *You* – do both.'

Two

Besides my 'brilliant' peers, I knew none of the other five in 6E1. A Black mop of hair – thirty maybe – sat at the back: not bad!

"Mr I'm-not-qualified" introduced "Black Mop's" name; not why he was there, move on! He called on my peers to dust the lustre of McCartney's lyrics. Sure.

When finished, Mr I'm-not-qualified gushed like a geyser. I had Hadron Collider brain! Laura's and Nick's interpretations were accurate, if artless; mine something else! Uncharacteristically panicked, I foresaw more mocking isolation for dim-wittedness.

He at the front couldn't look at me but droned … contemptuously? Whatever, it loitered around his hairy handlebar. 'Now, *Miss* Lloyd, let's see what *you* can do.'

Cornered, I garnered my faculties and delivered to finish on the bell. *He* was already at the door. His forceful slam rattled walls in the senior's study two rooms away.

Alone, I descended stairs of one building, traversed quadrangles, and ascended stairs to shelter in another's library. What stopped me from immediately exposing the manipulative horror to the Principal? The crippling shame game; adrift in '*no one* wanting me there'.

Recess over, I departed the library's refuge. Mid-quadrangle, Black Mop trotted two arm's lengths beside me.

'Keep walking. Don't look at me but listen, please. I have set and marked first English papers for HSCs, undergraduate and masters papers. You! You can run rings around these people. Don't let 'em bring you down. Do you hear me? Don't ever let them bring you down.'

Was he there to assess *him?* Next week, Black Mop had gone, not *him*.

Two encounters too many and dreams demolished, it took motley decades to fathom and unblock the extent of damage that Mr I'm-not-qualified had spun. His artful and insidious blend of goodwill and cruelty followed me shroud-like into every space I have entered … occupied since. Sticks and stones, ha! It's words what can knock ya'.

No longer stunned, words are my power.

Biography

A Circuitous Route

by Anna Russell

MY NAME IS Oliver Drought Tibeaudo. From the name you might think me French and once we were. I was actually born in King's County, Ireland, what you young ones might call County Offaly. By fate, my wife, Bridget Boland, was from Queen's County, a king and a queen joined in holy matrimony. An Offaly and a Laois doesn't have the same ring.

I was one of eleven children and Bridget and I went on to have thirteen. My family was of note though many would say my contribution to world history lacked significance. I beg to differ, but more on that later.

My ancestor, John Tibeaudo esq (alias Jean Thibaudeau) fled from France to Nova Scotia for refuge in the 1680s when the Edict of Nantes was revoked. He was, of course, a Huguenot. He then emigrated to Ireland leaving behind in Canada a selection of Tibeaudos, one of whom, Joseph, was Governor of Quebec. Another Joseph, my own father, was Commissary General in Ceylon.

I am licensee of the Star Hotel, Wagga Wagga.

My name appeared in print many times. Once when I identified a gentleman called Raymond Layard whose body was found floating in the Murrumbidgee River. Mr Layard had been residing at the Star and foul play was suspected.

Once my name appeared in the local paper in relation to an adopted quail, that was fun.

In 1875 a notice appeared in the *Australian Town and Country Journal* that I had bought a property in the Lachlan District including five thousand sheep, horses, plant and store.

And in 1881, in the NSW Government Gazette, there was a notice concerning my, um, insolvency.

My great-great granddaughter is here to speak for me because in 1887, I 'succumbed to that terrible affliction of cancer of the tongue' and can therefore speak no more.

Annie Reilley
by Narelle Fernance

AN IRISH GREETING to you all. My name is Annie Reilley. These days you will find me near the top of the golden staircase, as the sun's rays penetrate the cavity of clouds floating across the western sky before sunset. Attached to my white cloak are white feathery wings, and a garland graces my head. Though I'm not sure if a halo is fitting, due to my earth-life being a somewhat boisterous affair.

I married my Ned in 1860. We immediately set off north on horseback, seeking the dream of land and horses. We worked on stations during the years on the wallaby, and glimpsed the mighty Clarence River with Ned astride his favourite bay, and me conveying our first three childa in a dray, pulled by Clumper.

Ah, what a day it was when we finally arrived on our own selection of land in the Spring of '74, to my new slab bush-hut built by Ned and his mates. We paused at our new farm gate with five cows, three calves, two pigs, two geese and sundry hens and chickens. The eldest of our then seven childa rode the four horses, with their Da leading the draft mare. Three more childa were to be born in following years.

Spuds and corn were planted on the creek flats, along with a lush growth of lucerne to be hayed for Winter. The farm lay in a horseshoe formed by the meeting of Stockyard and Smith Creeks, to flood periodically, replenishing the valuable soil. My dairy herd grew to thirty, to be milked by hand twice daily, the cream to be churned into butter.

Emus twisted their heads to stare through the cracks in the slab-hut before continuing on to pick among the fire embers. My daughters loved searching for the nests of the free-range turkeys and geese – one day to be startled by the challenge of a crocodile that had arrived up the creek-bank on the same quest. That unexpected reptile had, in fact, been brought down from Queensland by a drifter who worked on a nearby holding.

What great sing-alongs and story-tellings our family of twelve enjoyed around the outside kitchen fireplace. I may not have been able to write, but I could tell a bush yarn, mimicking all the voices, roars and screeches as required by the story-line.

I keep an interested eye on my ever extending family, and particularly a great-granddaughter, Narelle. Funny ... she reminds me of me. Not only short and round, but loves sharing a bush yarn.

Unsung Hero

by Brydie O'Shea

I rode an Unsung Hero once,
His hoof-falls drummed the beat.
He carried me jig-jogily
With iron on his feet.
I rode him where most fear to tread
Full laden down with tack.
With temper bad he pulled like mad
He was straight off the track.

That horse and I patrolled the streets
Of Redfern and Kings Cross
Round and round in Sydney town
Hock-deep in human loss.
He looked on down with much disdain
At crowds, foul-mouthed and coarse
And if police
Don't believe in Peace
Then what of a Mountie's horse?

I always felt cut-up for him.
He had much life to lease
But he ended here
bringing up the rear
At the New South Wales Police.
That's how his days were endless filled

With brawls and kicks and biting
And scum-bag-fleas
Down-on-their-knees
While in the ghettos fighting.

He should have had the glory
Of the squadron lines extended.
An ANZAC horse that charged with force
Beersheba's Wells defended.
Instead, he dealt with junkies
And the lowest of the low
The murderers
And perjurers
Ignoblest of foe.

He should have had the fanfare
Of a ticker-tape parade.
Instead like lead I bowed my head
And sobbed upon his grave.
The years have passed so swiftly by
I've lost all track of time.
But that old hack
Gleaming black as black
Was some partner in crime.

I could not stem the hurt inside
The day his spirit flew
How can I explain?

It stabbed like knife pain.

I've had lovers far less true.

Warrigal.

Unsung Hero Horse.

Your picture hangs high on my wall.

Oh, the song was sweet

when they shod your feet

and we rode sixteen hands tall.

Hook, Line 'n' Sinker

by D'Arcy Lloyd

WHAT PART DID William Valentine play in Captain John Stein's life and death at 30 in 1841? Was the former's sensational saga of a shipwreck survival the whole truth and nothing but, or one of Valentine's fictitious cocktails with a dash of fact to suit his ends?

Deeply unpalatable but true, Australia was not just established on the backs of sheep, but whales. In September 1840, three-masted 250-ton whaling vessel *Mary* departed Port Jackson for waters east of New Guinea. It was Stein's fourth captaincy of the *Mary* following a decade of masterful navigational and captaincy achievements.

In 1832, at 22, Stein undertook, with five illiterate crew, 'The most daring circumnavigation of the globe's (Southern Ocean)' in a tiny 37-ton sloop. His commission? A lucrative cargo of coffee and tobacco from Rio de Janeiro. All returned hale 'n' hearty to Hobart within nine months. In 2024, Stein's achievement remains astonishing.

Mary's 1840 voyage was notably Valentine's first! What training, whaler or sailor, equipped him to recount four years later, in eloquent mariner's detail, *Mary's* disintegration at the Laughlan Islands during the 'ever memorable typhoon of December 1840'? Why subsequently would Laughlan and later Murua Islanders randomly 'massacre' Valentine's crew mates while welcoming him, only to spear him repeatedly over a period of three years, yet not kill him?

In November 1844, Valentine seized an opportunity to be discovered by whaler *Woodlark* and subsequently be transferred to *Tigress*, returning to Australia. *Tigress's* doctor confirmed his wounds were indisputable. However, Captain Eury affirmed his '... firm belief of the bloody tragedy transacted; but of the causes that led to it I am sceptical, particularly the first massacre on Laughlan Island, after having lived in friendly intercourse with the natives for a period of nine months.'

Was Eury compelled to dilute many of Valentine's barely plausible accounts? Were Sydney's masses intoxicated by the tale's macabre 'gone native' exotica to dispel suspicion? Though a conundrum today, Valentine's story warrants review, to honour all of *Mary's* 32 perished crew, and Stein who was proclaimed '... probably one of the most romantic marine figures ... Australia's colonies ... produced.'

Opening the Envelope

Valentine Lost

by D'Arcy Lloyd

Diary: Saturday, 25th March 1843

OH, MY LOST, darling husband. For five days and nights I have betrayed our bond to fill these pages for you, as I have since your departure nine hundred and eighteen days ago. I now bear a churning foggy paralysis, knowing that 'lost' is now the condition our daughter Eliza and I must forever know you.

My dearest John, I lament that your *'bravest sailor girl's'* anchor has failed us when most required. Though bereft, I return for I must write to you still as if awaiting your return.

Since your schooner sailed from Port Jackson on the 22nd September 1840, you and I have skimmed every nautical mile of the calm spring waters. Oh, how I sailed, Captain's daughter, Captain's wife, captain she. By the second year, we began to beat against the swells until in this third year I have plummeted and flung about in the ocean's fury, clinging to those indomitable futile spasms of hope.

I recall you speaking kindly of Captain McCarroll. I speak now in kind for it was he who coursed onto Laughlan Islands where the typhoon cast your fate. He rushed to me your few possessions retrieved from that coral isle where your hosts showed him, with honour, their grave for you. Your letters – concealed and seals intact – have miraculously come home. Though the script has faded, all is legible.

How my heart erupts in seizures from your coded words. You ask, should you have heeded my views on Mr Valentine? Though it grieves me that your Journal has not come, I will indulge hope eternally for its return. Rest in peace my beloved, your clues suffice, I will remain vigilant to Valentine's return then take your evidence to law.

Eternal love,

Sarah.

The Escape

by Barbara Maxwell

LIFE WAS THE same each day, helping milk the cows, housework with Elsie telling Jessie what to do, always bossing her. Resentment was growing but there was nowhere to go, what could she do? Jessie's primary school education was insufficient to qualify her for anything other than domestic work, and she most certainly did not want to do that!

Twenty-one soon and no future. The house was so empty with her brothers now in the army or on their own farms and all her sisters married bar her and Elsie. The local dances had stopped as the war progressed, and Elsie had become more domineering than ever. How she wished her beloved mother was still with them. Going to town in the Chev with Father was the highlight of the week.

This time, in the local paper, Jessie had noticed information about a nurse's entrance exam to be conducted at the Base Hospital and she thought maybe, she could sit that, it didn't state any educational standard. She had always been the top student in primary school, perhaps she could pass, leave the farm and Elsie.

Father drove her into the exam, expressing his disapproval. Jessie was terrified, it was so different to her one-teacher school as she entered the examination room at the hospital. Afterwards, Father collected her, and they drove home in silence.

Weeks later, the letter arrived, Jessie retreated to the shed behind the house to open it. So many thoughts flashed through her mind, images of her in a crisp white uniform only to be replaced with a future of drudgery here at the farm. Her hands were shaking, success would bring such possibilities, a new beginning, daunting but exciting. She tore open the envelope, a pass, acceptance to train at the hospital starting in the new year.

Father begged her not to go, promising to teach her to drive. Jessie refused all enticements and prepared herself to embark on this new life, naïve, excited and free.

Code Name: Envelope

By Chris McIntosh

'FINAL TESTING IS complete. All systems are live. We are green across the board. Awaiting confirmation.'

A group of civilians sat along a wide bench, facing a wall of monitors covered in graphs, diagrams and live video feeds. Behind them stood five older men in immaculate military uniforms. Their faces were expressionless, but one of them kept checking his watch. Another man stood in front of all of them, a red phone held to his ear. He waited for a while before speaking two words: 'Yes. Understood.' Then he nodded.

'Confirmation received. Go, go, go. We are opening The Envelope in three ... two ... one ...'

A button was pressed.

Three of the monitors showed different views of a large concrete platform in an otherwise featureless desert. Around the stage was a vast collection of electrical equipment. For a few moments nothing on screen seemed to change, then a small plume of dust or smoke gathered. The plume quickly grew into a swirling, violent cloud, sparks and flames roaring out of it. Electricity arced out of the cloud onto some of the equipment and the video on two of the screens flickered. Then out of the maelstrom stepped a giant humanoid figure, four or five metres tall. Shaped like a man, but with brightly glowing eyes, the thing spoke with a booming voice.

'Menn yedg-erro arla iss-aarga no-mee?'

A dark-skinned woman at the bench gasped loudly, and covered her face with shaking hands. She muttered and cried – possibly praying, definitely panicking.

'What the hell is that?' shouted one of the generals, though he already knew. 'What did it say?' The figure reacted, looking directly into the main camera as if it could see them down here in their deep bunker.

'Who dares disturb my slumber?'

One of the civilians fainted. Everyone else sat or stood silently, not quite believing what they were seeing, not knowing if they should be celebrating or terrified.

One hundred metres above them, between the creature's enormous feet, sat a small, unassuming brass lamp.

Dear Judith

by Anna Russell

Dear Judith,

We have terrible news. Our Julie, our dear girl, never came home to us but has died in Tibet. Remember when you so kindly visited our home to bring the presents she had given you for us, we told you that we'd had a telephone call from her that day and that she was stuck in Lhasa with altitude sickness. She never did make it to Kathmandu for three days later, on Christmas morning, we had a telegram from her friend saying she had died. Of course we wanted to go to her straight away and bring her home, but this was not possible and she was cremated. She is with us, however, on the mantlepiece, and we are glad to have her. The government also arranged for her belongings to be shipped to us. We couldn't believe how heavy her rucksack was, how did she carry it around?

Now, my dear, we know that you only spent a few days with her but she was very fond of you, she told us so. We wanted to give you a small keepsake, to remember her by. Sadly, her camera was missing from her bag but we did find a few rolls of film which we had developed. One of them had a lovely photo of the two of you, on the ferry we think, so we are enclosing a copy. We also found this little stone lion and thought you might like it too.

Our doctor said that the illness you both had on the ferry may have made the altitude sickness much worse. We hope that you have recovered completely as you still had a cough when you were here. And Judith, next time you are in England, do please come and see us.

With God's blessings, Rose and Patrick Deadman.

Tearaway

Lasseter's Reef
by Brydie O'Shea

Here are things I need to say (the cat near
Got my tongue).
There's no poetic justice when the jury's hung?
I have bitten off the bullet;
Got the lead out of my gun.
The past is gone; cannot
Be changed. What's
Done is done is done.

I wish that you had voiced it at
'Speak now or hold your
Peace.' But you turned
Back. You cast
First stone. You
Killed the golden geese.
The sun has been struck from
The day. The gild gone
From the fleece.
The golden nugget you gave
Me was mixed at
Lasseter's Reef.

You have the heart of
Gemini. You're Janus
At the gate.
Your sweetness was a
Sugar-high. Our love up
For debate.
You double-dealt. You stabbed
My back. You practiced
With Hecate.
I laugh, since our infinity's
A fallen sideways eight.

Do you know how hard it was
To tearaway
From you?
It should have not
Been half as hard
Since you were
Never true.
Well, I'm the fool not
Holding gold, and quartz
Runs through my veins.
Your iron pyrite dazzled
Me, reflecting off the plains

You (in my mind) were
golden; formed by exploding stars
I thought our love was heavenly.

Passed Jupiter and Mars.

You taught me not to hurt again;

I learnt from your terse brief.

The golden nugget you gave

Me, came from Lasseter's Reef.

An Apprentice for Thunderbolt

by Narelle Fernance

I WAS LYING relaxed, leaning against my saddle, Combo tethered patiently nearby, warm sun shining intermittently between the gum leaves waving idly in the breeze. I could hear him clambering up the hillside towards me. He was probably doing his best to do such silently, but with moving shale, dry leaves and twigs, providence was against him. Combo had heard him, of course, and had given a low warning whinny.

Suddenly the youth sprung past the last rock and stood there in front of me, grinning. I had observed him through still half-closed eyes but had returned to my relaxed ruse.

'Excuse me Sir, do you know where I might find Thunderbolt?' The lad was fairly dancing from one foot to the other, shoulders rising and falling.

'Why would you be looking for Thunderbolt?' I replied, looking him squarely in the eye. 'He's that ruthless killer bushranger that we have all heard about. Why would a young kid, still wet behind the ears, better suited to be by your mother's side, be interested in finding Thunderbolt?'

'Oh no Sir, Thunderbolt is not a ruthless killer, he's the gentleman bushranger that has a fun-filled life, robbing rich old men, partying at the inns, complimenting the ladies and laughing with his friends. I want to be his apprentice, learn to do what he does, instead of being at home where my stepfather belts me, and my mum. Then he locks me in the dunny for hours if I don't get all the work done.'

'Do you know how dangerous bushranging is? Traps hounding you everywhere you go, never knowing peace?' I roared at him to dissuade his ambitions.

'You are Thunderbolt! I knew it!' he grinned. 'Yes I reckon I'm up for it. Nothing is as bad as being at home with my stepfather.'

'You are a bit of a tearaway, aren't you. Go home and sleep on it. Be back at dawn if you don't change your mind.'

At the crack of dawn, Will Monckton was back on his best mangy horse. His bright eyes and wide grin announcing his enthusiasm to get started as Thunderbolt's apprentice.

Dusty

by Kris Nissam

SHE WAS A real tearaway; you couldn't get near her if she didn't want you there. She would circle around with a wary look on her face, but always intrigued by what you were doing.

She had blonde hair with a long face, pointy nose and intelligent brown eyes. She could run like the wind and circle around behind you in a flash. Typical of a teenager. She would say hello if it suited her or totally ignore you on any other day.

On other occasions she would be your best friend and sit remarkably close, never wanting to leave.

I wondered about her upbringing being one of seven. She was the only female, and the resulting light colouring compared to her brother's dark complexions and black hair made me ponder her background.

She was a great co-worker, with foresight into impending situations and ready to back up the team. Always ready to work unless the temperature reaches 40 degrees. On these occasions you would find her in the pool or languidly lazing, dripping wet beside it.

People admired her agility and speed, her intelligent looks and lithe figure. She protected her home and surroundings with due diligence and was always on the lookout for the whole team. You would know in a short space of time if you were an acceptable person in her surmising. Her voice and tone would attest to that.

Well despite being the tearaway that she was, when the chips were down or there was an incident at hand, she seemed to sense that now was not the time for theatrics.

Such as when the long, shiny black snake appeared at the tap and slithered under the diesel tank and up into the tractor bucket.

She jumped and danced about; the high-pitched bark alerted me!

That's my Dusty dog. GOOD GIRL!

Impact

by Chris McIntosh

THE SUNGLASSES WERE cheap, and the jacket was plastic rubbish, but there was a pile of unopened mail on top so he grabbed that before closing the door and continuing down the street. The owner probably wouldn't even notice it was missing, until they got home.

It was mostly bills. He was doing them a favour, really. The heavily-tattooed young man stopped at the first bin and tossed the invoices into it. A quick look at the bank statements showed that the tight-arsed Mazda driver could afford better clothes. And a better car.

There were several catalogues. A flyer from some mob claiming that QR codes were the mark of the beast. Two birthday cards – one from 'Mum', one from 'Aunty Sarah'. Sarah's twenty dollars went straight in his pocket.

'Thanks, Aunty Sarah!' he said cheerfully, as the cards joined everything else in the trash. An Asian woman walking by frowned at him. 'Aunty Sarah always remembers me birthday!' The woman looked away as she passed.

His phone made a very loud, distinctly female moan. A text message from a mate, wanting some weed. He ignored it. He had twenty bucks burning a hole in his jeans, and KFC was just around the corner.

Before he made it to the corner, though, a man walked out of a shop in front of him – and he felt the world tilt sideways. His stepfather, right there, walking towards him. Without even realising, he touched a hand to his side, to the ribs that had long healed but would never truly heal. He'd stopped breathing. He couldn't think. His mind was an angry swarm of bees, stinging him, stinging itself. Nothing made sense.

The man who slightly resembled his stepfather passed him without a glance. His actual stepfather had been dead for years. No longer hungry, he turned and headed for home. Stopping at the unlocked Mazda, he opened the passenger door and threw Sarah's twenty dollars on the seat.

Lost

by Anna Russell

October 13: Chennai

Today, Ingrid asked me to leave. I was expecting and dreading it, was only supposed to stay a week and it's been a month. I don't know what to do but Chennai is too expensive for me now.

October 14: Mahabalipurum

Bought a ticket for the first bus leaving this morning and now I'm here, writing by the light of the little LED I keep in my pocket as there are no light bulbs in this windowless room. I have a bathroom though even if the hot tap gives me electric shocks and the water dribbles out of the wall rather than the shower head. At least I was able to wash my backpack which brought the smell of old fish with it from the bus. Rain endless, gutters overflowing.

October 15:

Found phone kiosk and called home. Asked mum for money and she said yes then dad got on and said no, that he would send a plane ticket to Chennai instead. Come home Son, he said, your mother's very worried. He sounded like he was crying. Went for walk on beach to check out possibility of camping but too many losers like me already doing that. Girl in coffee house told me about an ashram 100 kms west. Will go tomorrow.

October 16:

Guy at ashram looked me up and down but let me stay. He said they operate on donations but as I can't pay I must contribute by cleaning toilet block. He gave me a bunk in the dormitory.

Christmas Day:

Same as any other. Have graduated to cleaning the hall. New people all the time. Can't afford to call home, the kiosk in the village only accepts rupees and I have none. Feeling untethered and hopeless, trapped. Meditation gives little peace.

Farewell – Flights of Fancy

by D'Arcy Lloyd

PICTURE PEAK HOUR 1953 and a treacherously steep arterial city road.

Our mother was engaged in affairs of commerce when a thing zipped at low altitude past our peripheral vision. Seconds later, traffic jammed, frantic witnesses rushed, and Mum's fleeting curiosity erupted in primal fear!

Astonished onlookers described Tris's 'arms and legs akimbo', and expressions some said were terror! Others? Sheer ecstasy!

Then, one tabloid sensationally launched 'the legend' with:

TEARAWAY TODDLER'S

tricycled flight of fancy!

Fully recovered, Tristan insisted on fairy's wings! Dad skulled a double cognac or two, while Mum scoffed, 'He'll get past it soon enough.'

Rest assured, the fairy's-wings, yes. Not the obsession!

Tris then moved on to plummeting from heights strapped to improvised eiderdowns and wailing, 'CX4 to control!' Needless to add, cries of, 'Call an ambulance!' accompanied Tris throughout his youth, and the GP's gentle calls – always – to Mother sighed, 'Now, I don't want you to worry old thing, but …'

In recoveries, Tris obsessively read Biggles and recited it verbatim … ad nauseum.

The next less-dangerous obsession involved precious squadrons of model aircraft. Tiger Moths, Mustangs, Sabre and Mirage battled it out beneath Tris's intransigent 'must-have cerulean-blue' ceiling.

Fortunately, Dad's distress abated from Tearaway's tireless escapades, while Mum sustained her lyrical staccato refrain, 'Better fanciful flights than fights, dear.'

At sixteen, Tris was airborne unrestricted in a Cessna 150. Within five years he was cruising at Mach Two's in FA-18s, and latterly F-35 Lightnings.

Congrats to our parents for indulging and enduring Tris's determined dreams, despite some stratospheric medical bills. Rounds of applause, too, to the RAAF for entrusting him with eye-wateringly expensive jets.

Group Captain – callsign Tearaway – you *lucky* man, you have flown faster, higher, freer than us all! This farewell is your final clearance to land. Good luck in retirement.

Sans E

Autumn Rain
by Chris McIntosh

WAS IT ALWAYS raining? It's raining again now. I can't think of a day it didn't. Not that I'm complaining, but too much of a good thing can turn into ... too much. I'm standing and watching, through a foggy window, on this brisk autumn morning. Rain on iron roof, on grass and paving – low drumming, splashing, monotonous and cold. Drops run slowly down frigid glass that I don't want to touch. I burrow into my fluffy gown.

Birds stalk around on soggy lawn, still hunting bugs and worms notwithstanding damp conditions. I ask my vacant living room if birds know cold, or any discomfort. Do sparrows worry about storms, larks avoid lightning or a finch flinch from booming clouds? Important inquiry! But no word of a solution. Assiduous about food, though. Hop, look, jab – a mouthful of brunch.

An abrupt storm hit last night, with blossom and sticks now adorning my frost-brown yard. Luckily nothing too harsh. It will all grow back in spring. I'll mow on a warm day in August and that will tidy up most of it quick smart. I'm not going out to pick it up today.

Soft footfalls, arms around my waist, and a warm body against my back. 'What you doing?'

'Watching rain, and hungry birds.'

'It's cold.'

'It is.'

'I'm kinda hungry too …'

I turn around. 'Is that so? What can I–'

A hard kiss from soft lips. Oh. *That* sort of hungry.

Autumn rain can wait. So can thoughts of storms and parrots and jobs outdoors. I put my mug on a window sill. Hand in hand, back to our room. I know that two of us can think of ways to stay warm.

Lip Service

by D'Arcy Lloyd

A PANGRAMMATIC LIPOGRAM? Without a what! Our most ubiquitous sound. Why?

Who would inform any animals to abstain from that natural sound? From primordial hominoids on, all animals grunt in vocoids from ah to 'i' to 'o' to 'u' without ignoring a 'taboo no sound', from:

Sucking, purring, hissing, and roaring.

Mooing, yapping, woofing and growling.

M-a-a-a-a-aing and baaing.

Hoot hooting and chirruping.

Huffing and … now I'm puffing!

What is missing? Apply your scholarly mind, imagination or auditory skills, or toss it off and walk away, though it is curious. For

today, on command, I must omit our most ubiquitous sound for …
for what?

Infants, ignorant of lipogrammic sports, won't stop from blurting playful joyful sounds of ahs, oohs and ughs. But wait, our most shrill toot is missing for I must abstain.

Was Mr Wright's *'Gadsby'* vain for boldly and mockingly inscribing his lipogrammic story with words containing a 'taboo no sound', only to abolish it from fifty thousand plus words that follow? What was his point? Was his goal a worthy pursuit or diminishing? Who knows, or could?

Can audiologists, phonologists or musicians omit any natural sound from study or application? If so, why? Should actors, journalists, and authors?

I think not and though not phonologist or audiologist, I am a musician, though a lazy-lapsing kind, and I am an author and thus will not brook or tarry.

A Moonlight Meeting

by Narelle Fernance

'I WAS RIDING in and out of hill spurs, through thick shrub,' Ward is saying. 'Combo is watching, sniffing air, and allows a whinny, knowing a human is awaiting our arrival. Within a moon-cast shadow I sight a mortal against a burnt-out stump. I stop, watching all surroundings for a trap, for a trap looks similar to a patrolman, only in casual clothing.

'As I approach, gaining no confirmation of a trap, I am conscious of Martin Quigly, who had shown only good human warmth on that disastrous hold-up at Bylong. At that locality Mary Ann and I did our last job. Though awfully ill, Mary Ann was still firm on tactics. On that occasion, Quigly had thought that I should abandon any hold-up plan and was vastly trusting with a small book of his containing many pounds for us, notwithstanding.'

'I stop a short span from him, touching my shirt front, confirming that I am carrying a sum of cash to pay that account back to Quigly. But I doubt that is why Quigly is now standing in moonlight in front of us,' Ward adds, thinking back to that Bylong situation.

'I would think your hair was standing up on your scruff a bit,' says Sam. 'Martin Quigly may not want his cash, but a squadron of law making humans possibly thought it was good to point guns at you from bush surrounding that moon-lit gap.'

'That is so,' said Ward. 'But I didn't think that of Martin Quigly, who was calmly walking towards us. I was musing that I should dismount and stand with Combo, as Quigly was approaching, with his hand out, off'ring only sympathy for my Mary Ann's passing.'

Darwinism of Words
by Brydie O'Shea

Words

First form in minds of

Fish.

Crawling on

Land.

Trying to talk to groups of distant

Fish.

moving forward

And looking up

At sounds of wind

And bird-flight-hums

In thick, dark woods

That fish did

Climb.

Grow fur

And torso pound.

And opposingly

Play tricks

Of hand

And thumbs.

'Tis a sapling hour of Words.

Of grunts

And groans

And nods

And touch.

No form; still dumb.

Man climbs

Down.

Stands

Up.

Fights dark with

Burns.

Draws dog with

Food

And hunts.

Man from his soul

Calls to Gods.

Forms

Words.

From symbols cast in

Rock.

And oaths

Of honour

Sworn

And writ in

Blood.

Around this point.

Young Plato

Talks

To Glaucon

Of Atlantis

Lost

And in all his fiction

says…

'Wisdom is

Knowing you know

Nothing.'

That old Socratic

Contradiction.

Words

From tiny

Atoms

Of basic

A.B.C.

Can cut

And blind

And build

Bring joy

And fight.

And stay a

Sword.

If said in vain,

Words

Count

Your worn-out striding to infinity.

Hold in your palm

And blow away.

Wizard word magic

Witch doll and clay

Alas

That our said 'Words'

Will no way

Unsay.

States of Play

Politics and Kelpies

by Narelle Fernance

THE 'STATE OF play'! Could we be referring to a country not far away, where a politician, known as the 'Clown' by many, survives an assassination attempt? Suddenly everyone is sympathetic and loves everybody else, forgetting all animosities. Then the opposing side's candidate, referred to by many as 'Doddery', makes a very delayed decision to pull out of the race. Two days later the shooting is forgotten, old animosities return, with both sides again derogatively referring to each other. But it is known the injured politician, now with the sympathy vote, will be impossible to beat. The opposing side run a 'lame duck' to retain their woke stature, for they know the injured one will win the election, but he will then not be eligible to run for the top job again. That will be when the opposing side has the opportunity to pull out their 'wild card', to mop up the resultant mess. The country will probably survive, but will the World? That is 'the state of play' on the big scale.

Or can the 'state of play' be as simple as my two kelpies challenging each other over a bone? Big Kelpie has the bone and places it just far enough away to entice Little Kelpie to try to snatch it. Big Kelpie watches very closely with eagle eye. On first indication of Little Kelpie being tempted, Big Kelpie growls and snaps. Little Kelpie settles back in crouch. Big Kelpie grabs bone, charges around in a maniacal circle, replaces bone, waiting, enticing! The one-sided play is repeated and repeated. Little Kelpie feigns disinterest! Big Kelpie gets bored and turns body ever so slightly, in order to scratch an ear. Little Kelpie, quick as a wink, grabs bone and runs. Straight as a die under the ute, then chewing contentedly, knowing Big Kelpie can't get her there!

Both scenarios have so much in common!

A Lifetime at the Beach

by Kris Nissam

WATCH THE BABY crawling towards the sea, full of intent and awe. Probably reminiscent of the womb, warm comforting environment, floating and swimming without a care.

Then a toddler jumping waves, whether they're wearing bathers in Victoria, swimmers in NSW or togs in Queensland, it makes no difference. The enjoyment the laughter and the leap of faith over the waves is still the same.

The young child building a castle fit for a princess, decorated with shells and seaweed, promptly destroyed by an older sibling. But as he falls backwards into the hole that was dug to build the castle, a karmic response is enacted on the east coast of Australia.

The child learning to work with nature and read the waves, until success is achieved by body surfing to the shore. Only to be repeated again and again with every chance to be in the ocean.

Teenagers surfing with the first surfboard, leg rope attached and the indescribable feeling of cutting through the surf, powered by the force of nature. Local knowledge and unspoken laws revered. Exhilarating days and near-death experiences. But, oh so much fun.

An adult, swimming in and out, a mild reprieve from the everyday concerns, thoughts and worries. A state of pure bliss, recharging and gentle thoughts.

Older adults marvelling at the bubbles on the shore and the sheer strength of the waves these days, no matter which state it's just the temperature that varies.

Birthday greetings etched into the sand, to photograph and send to friends and family interstate. A simple uncomplicated and free activity that brings so much joy and shared understanding.

Ashes spread into the sea, a joyful reunion with those that have gone before. Salty tears, releasing fears, because evolution decrees that we will all eventually reach this state of play.

This Unholy Alliance

by D'Arcy Lloyd

JOHN'S BUOYANT GREETING dances across spring morning's hue. He's asking if I'm intent on striding out apace; his familiar question, his invitation.

Content in the octogenarian's company, I thank him and slow. This former practitioner of striding out apace, now cedes reluctantly to his ailing body's demise.

At the park, we sit, each absorbed in the cosmos. I venture to assert, 'We are lovers of peace with nature at dawn, John … chronotypically lions.'

He smiles, nods knowingly and affirmatively. Though silence returns, it's certainly not for poverty of thoughts.

His voice, on returning, proves uncharacteristically thorny. 'Play up! Play up!' and questions, 'And play the game?' Abandoning protest, he engages with, 'You do know it?'

Relieved not to disappoint, I confirm, 'Newbolt? Yes.'

I anticipate a recitation, or request! Apparently satisfied, he smiles and returns to morning's atmosphere. Though my mind traverses a jumble of conversational pathways, I wait for John's lead.

He recalls delicious dreams of leather on willow, and fuzzy rubber balls bouncing off catgut strings. He asks if I remember the sporting days of collective generosity and spirited goodwill that cared for the joy, not which side conquered.

'Oh! I do, John. Though regretfully, aggressive tribalism now sullies those joys, and is co-opted …'

He's jumped to conclude, '… by an unholy alliance, yes! From sport to commerce, parliaments to international intercourse. It so permeates every crevice; we can't tell one from the other today.'

'You are reading my mind, John!'

We walk again, ambling. At his gate, his palpable pain ignites within a sorrowful lament. 'These corrupted states of play are the winters of all our discontents, and we humans have certainly lost our way. This might be our River Styx!'

Becalmed again, he bids farewell and departs, optimistically humming Imagine!

The Fool's Journey

by Brydie O'Shea

I read the true deck and you're a Fool.
A Joker, near journey's end.
My heart was never yours, my love.
To bruise and break and bend.

I see the future through tear-filled-eyes.
In empty cups of tea.
The Lover in your Tarot cards.
Was someone else than me.

I wished you Wheels of Fortune.
The Stars. The Sun. The Moon.
But my Love, I know of her.
It's written on each rune.

Just a Fool upon your journey
Don't think you'll find The World, my love.
Just regrets for yesterday.
Just a wild card gone astray.

I thought our love would last
Always.
But that's not quite
The State of Play.
Tomorrow's now
It's Devil's Day.

And I don't need no card to tell you.

You won't find love like ours again.

And I predict you'll wish you hadn't.

Washed me away in desert rain.

Bad Actors

By Chris McIntosh

TWO MEN SAT in low-backed armchairs, next to an open fire that was a little too wide for the size of the room. The chairs had deep buttons and polished leather, and a small coffee table sat between them – the timber dark and ornately carved. Under their feet: the spotted fur of some exotic animal. The fire was the only light in the room, casting disfiguring shadows across the men's faces, yet neither felt its heat. They regarded each other impassively.

'What's the state of play?' asked the second man. His tone was almost bored, but his eyes were sharp.

The first took a sip from his tumbler, before answering.

'The President's two points down, but holding steady. Everything else is in place, with one exception.'

'Russia?'

'No. Distracted. China too. Venezuela took some manoeuvring, but they seem to be on track now.'

'So what do you need from us?'

The first man took another sip from his glass, then placed it on the table. He paused, possibly for dramatic effect, before speaking again.

'North Korea. We need Kim Jong Bae to murder his wife.'

The second man raised his eyebrows, but said nothing. He waited for more details but there were none forthcoming. He knew if he needed more information, it would have been provided. Free play, then. He lowered his eyebrows and swirled the drink in his own glass.

'Something like that is going to take some time to arrange. Give me a couple of hours. I'll make some calls.'

When the men returned later, neither spoke. There was no need. The second man nodded, to indicate the job had been done. The first also nodded: message received.

Both men vanished, then the virtual room ceased to exist – leaving no trace of the men, their identities or their conversation.

A week later, the war started.

Narelle Fernance

The majority of Narelle's contributions to this anthology are excerpts from her novel *To Those That Wait*, which challenges the theory that it was Fred Ward lying dead in the bloodied Kentucky Creek when Northern Tablelands bushranger, Thunderbolt, was shot in 1870. Her other novels are: *On Roads Most Travelled*, bringing to life the story of her Irish great-grandparents and their families who settled in the Upper Clarence Valley in the late 19th century; and *The Outback as Never Before or Since*, depicting a joyous romp across Australian deserts by three friends. More about Narelle and her readable yarns can be discovered at www.narelle-fernance.com

D'Arcy Lloyd

Strategic and analytical by nature, education and practice, it is no surprise that these traits have followed D'Arcy's late-life transition from corporate advice to creative writing. Long-term consequences of historical decisions made – or not – lie at the centre of D'Arcy's works-in-progress. Easily intrigued and captivated by fragments of facts, they leap out and seed D'Arcy's plausible – if not entirely factual – stories. Characters' lives interweave with the social, political, commercial, economic and creative prisms from the past to the present. D'Arcy's current major work in progress is an anthology of factional stories. Titled *The Waterloo Series*, it draws on fragments of historical facts from a celebrated rural station in the Matheson Valley of Australia's New England region. The anthology's title reflects the Station's name. To follow D'Arcy's progress, go to www.darcylloyd.com

Barbara Maxwell

Child, student, public servant, wife, mother, traveller, manager, organiser, taxi driver and finally a farmer. 'Maybe I'm even a writer, but it has been a blast!' she says.

Chris McIntosh

Chris has always wanted to tell stories. His parents met in a band, and he grew up an only child in a small country town – surrounded by creative people and with plenty of time and space to think, explore and dream. He has lived in coastal cities and the bush, and worked in graphic design and website development before returning to the family farm in northern NSW.

Kris Nissam

Kris's writing reflects on past events with humour, sadness and gratefulness. In doing that she hopes to promote optimistic reactions and endeavours to inspire future opportunities for all who care to read her stories.

Brydie O'Shea

Brydie is a north west NSW Angus beef farmer, wildlife carer and commercial native plant grower, activities which she often finds incompatible. Once in a far-off time she was a mounted policewoman, then a New Zealand zoo guide. Brydie is an animal tragic who lives with her husband Kelvin and their collection of contented creatures. Her short story Corona Australis appears in *Dark Sky Dreamings: an Inland Skywriters Anthology* and the *Outer Space, Inner Minds* anthology (both Interactive Publications). Her short story The Fates is published in *This Is Not A Horror Story* (Night Terror Novels), and her poem The Min Min Lights was longlisted for the Heroines Women's Writing Prize. Brydie always dreamed of being a published writer, but until now was bogged down by life.

Anna Russell

Anna's life has been bookended in northern New England. In between, curiosity has driven her to live in four different countries and to have countless careers, from archivist to Turkish hotelier. In 2020, she extended her creativity from visual artist to writer and now she can't stop, having written an historical novel, a collection of short stories, and two adult contemporary novels in the last five years. For more, go to judithannarussellcreative.com.au

High Country Books is an imprint of The Makers Shed

publishing a select range of fiction and non-fiction

www.themakersshed.org

*The High Country Books logo is based on a copper and sterling-silver brooch
created by Richard Moon Wearable Silver & Silverware. The design is derived from a
eucalyptus leaf, symbolising the well-forested mountains of Australia's high-altitude regions.*

www.ingramcontent.com/pod-product-compliance
Lightning Source LLC
Chambersburg PA
CBHW020530120726
47904CB00003B/1026